ALSO BY

TH

The Duke's Daughter ~ Lady Amelia Atherton

The Baron in Bath ~ Miss Julia Bellevue

The Deceptive Earl ~ Lady Charity Abernathy

THE BAGGINGTON SISTERS

The Countess and the Baron ~ Prudence

Almost Promised ~ Temperance

The Healing Heart ~ Mercy

The Lady to Match a Rogue ~ Faith

NETTLEFOLD CHRONICLES

Not Quite a Lady; Not Quite a Knight

Stitched in Love

THE HAWTHORNE SISTERS

The Forbidden Valentine ~ Lady Eleanor

CONTENTS

THE COUNTESS AND THE BARON

The Countess
and the Baron

Prudence

The Baggington Sisters

Isabella Thorne

A Regency Romance Novel

The Countess and the Baron ~ Prudence
The Nettlefold Chronicles ~ The Baggington Sisters

All rights reserved.

2018 Mikita Associates Publishing

Published in the United States of America.

www.isabellathorne.com

*M*iss Prudence Baggington's fine light brown hair had been arranged atop her head with a garland of minuscule white flowers that her maid called baby's breath. She still wore her dressing robe, but the voluminous folds of her wedding gown were draped over the edge of the bed and ready to be worn. She still could not quite believe that this day had arrived. She expected someone to come and snatch the victory away from her.

Outside her window, dawn colored the sky with the most beautiful array of red and orange sunbeams that Prudence had seen in weeks. She had thought to have once heard a saying about a crimson sky in the morning being a cause for alarm, but shook her head and laughed at the silly, childish notion.

Of course there was nothing more beautiful than a rose-hued sunrise. The weather was beautiful and she was about to be wed. At last. She let herself breathe in the cool scent of the morning and sighed with relief.

Marriage. Escape was perhaps a better word, but marriage would do. Once married she would be safe. She had dreamed of little else for most of her life, and she had prayed most dearly for these past few years. At last her prayers were answered, though not in the way she expected.

Of course Prudence did not want to stay on as a spinster in her father's home. Perish the thought. Still she had thought her groom would have been the wealthy and oh so handsome Duke of Kilmerstan, but Garrett Rutherford had evaded her every move, and eventually married that little mouse of a woman, Juliana Willoughby.

Prudence huffed. Juliana was on the shelf for years. How could she have succeeded where Prudence failed? The thought still irritated but Prudence pushed it from her mind. She could not be bothered by that now. It was her wedding day.

She may not be marrying a duke, but an earl would certainly do. She would be a countess. That status had to count for something. A bit of cheer bubbled in to halt her consternation. She would make all the hypocritical biddies who called her "the baggage" eat their words. She smiled at the thought, took up her wedding dress, and twirled around the room. She could not ever remember being so happy. She smiled at herself in the glass.

"Yes, Countess," she said. "Right away, Countess."

She carefully hung the gown again. It was true that her situation was not what she had once hoped, but there was good in it, she thought. One unexpected kiss of passion with a near stranger, an earl no less, had led to the marriage arrangement and the reading of the banns.

She had expected each Sunday to have someone object to her impending marriage, but looking around the church she saw no one speak to oppose it, not even the Earl of Fondleton himself.

At first, Prudence had been nervous about the marriage and about the earl's absence at each reading of the banns, but the happy day had arrived. Marriage to an earl had not been her plan, but he was titled, and wealthy. He was not old, nor was he terrible to look at. What more could a lady ask? They would grow to know and love each other in time. She was sure of it. Certainly, this was a better option than her current situation.

She shuddered.

The truth was that Prudence would have married just about anyone to get out of her father's house. She, and her mother, had been plotting for months to catch eligible gentlemen in the Nettlefold countryside, but all to no avail. No expense had been spared. They had ordered the most extravagant gowns and perfumes to catch the attentions of the gentlemen. Prudence had been hesitant at first to follow the advice of a London socialite, but her mother paid heavily for the designs, so Prudence capitulated.

She had shrugged her shoulders and gone along with the ploy, even attempting to enact an overly feminine accent that she had been instructed would appeal to the gentlemen's ears. She thought she sounded akin to a banshee, but the gentlemen did take notice. Still, it was a relief to know that she could return to her normal tone, even if some said she had a voice like a man. Perhaps speaking normally would bring an end to the hoarseness and sore throat which plagued her in the mornings.

Prudence had thought all the glitter and glam a farce, but perhaps her mother was right. Perhaps such maneuverings worked. After all, the machinations did end with her engagement. She would be Lady Fondleton.

"Lord and Lady Fondleton," she had whispered to herself in the mirror as the hope for her future lay ahead in an endless road of promise. While their meeting had been abrupt and, of course, improper, there was some romance to it as well. One could not be kissed in a stable without the thought of romance, she supposed.

She brought her fingers to her lips, remembering. The kiss was rather abrupt and rough, but she supposed the earl had not thought so well of her at the time. He did not know she was a lady. In the dark he seemed to think her someone else, perhaps a kitchen wench or some drab. She would not censure him, she decided, if he wanted to take a mistress, as long as he was discreet and she was with child first. He would want an heir, of course. She tapped her fingers nervously with the thought. She remembered the first and only time she had met her soon-to-be husband.

Upon literally bumping into one another in the stables of the Inn, Prudence had nearly fallen off balance. She was sure she wind milled her arms in a most unbecoming way, and her hat had fallen askew, but instead of being put off by her unladylike stance, the man caught her. Overcome with passion in that moment, he had swept down upon her, gathered her close to his very masculine form and planted a hard kiss upon her lips.

She had not been prepared. Never before had she felt quite so overwhelmed. She had perhaps just this once earned the nickname of baggage, because she was so thrilled in the moment, that she had not decried his boldness. Instead, she had allowed the kiss. Well, she supposed she did not really have a choice in the matter. She did not even have time to be afraid.

He had her in his arms, one hand laced through her hair and the other clasped her to him in a very ungentlemanly way. She should have been afraid. He was so audacious and overwhelmingly male, she found herself as meek as a kitten. She could not even utter a squeak. Such was not a disposition that others expected of Prudence – lioness perhaps, or jackal, but not kitten. She was certain that the earl's passionate kiss had been a sign of their destined future, and then they were well and truly caught.

Once caught in such an embrace there had been no explaining it. Prudence had swooned in his arms and he had held her. He had kissed her quite thoroughly and she imagined that she looked quite flushed and disheveled with the whole affair when Mrs. Hardcastle came upon them and exclaimed her outrage. She couldn't even blame Mrs. Hardcastle for outing them. After all, the woman knew Prudence was contending for a husband. Mrs. Hardcastle knew her situation, and she saw a solution. Prudence took it. Perhaps she should thank the woman.

Prudence twirled a recalcitrant curl around her finger, tucking it into place.

Perhaps the earl loved her, Prudence thought suddenly. She wondered, could it be love at first sight on his behalf? She could only hope that love might grow between them, but no matter. It would be better than home. She had to believe that.

Still, as the passion of their wedding night approached, Prudence could not help but worry. She remembered the earl's embrace. It had not been full of love, but full of lust. She shuddered with the thought, but she reminded herself, she would be his wife. She would have stature.

He was simply overcome with passion in the stable. He would not treat his wife so callously. On their wedding night she was sure he would apologize for his previous behavior, and she would forgive him. He would be her husband and offer her his protection. She would suffer his embrace. This she could do.

He would be more caring this time, she thought. He would be gentler and gentlemanly. She had thought of little else but the wedding night for weeks prior to today, though she had never had the opportunity to be alone with her betrothed. In fact, she had not seen the earl at all. If she were not currently looking at her wedding finery, she would have wondered if this was really the morning of her nuptials.

Father would walk her down the aisle. With any luck this would be the last time the man would touch her. She remembered Father's reaction when the news of her indiscretion reached him. He was, as was to be expected, furious. But after today, his wrath would not be able to touch her. She would be under her husband's protection. She smiled.

Prudence was just pleased to have escaped her father's grasp once and for all. Now, with a wealthy husband, she could lead the sort of life that she, and her many sisters, had always dreamed of. Her sisters. She would allow them all to visit as often as they could. She would shelter them. She would not abandon them like her older sister Temperance had done, running off to a convent rather than marrying. No. She, Prudence, would help them, just as soon as she was married to the earl.

"Mama," Prudence had called. "I am ready."

Her mother had entered the room with a smile as bright as the rising sun.

"You shall be beautiful," she whispered into her daughter's curls.

Prudence bit her lip. With several sisters well known for their timeless beauty and remarkable features, Prudence was more than aware of her plain face. Plump cheeks and a voluptuous frame softened any definable structure that was applauded in the willow thin bodies of her siblings. Even her eyes were nothing that would cause prose to be written in the throes of passion and love. Brown. Brown. Brown. Nothing more, nothing less. There was nothing special about her, Prudence thought. It was for that reason that she had allowed her mother to doll her up in extravagant costumes that might help her to stand out amongst the crowd of beautiful debutantes.

As Prudence stepped into her wedding gown, which

was soon pulled tight by her mother's practiced fingers, she began to worry.

"Mama," she whispered. "Lord Fondleton... he is a good man, is he not?"

"He is an earl," her mother replied as if that were all the answer needed.

Prudence thought on her mother's words for a long while. Titled gentlemen were expected to be above all others in regard to their morality and character. Still... she wondered. He seemed nice enough. He offered plenty of smiles and compliments, but so did her father. In public, he seemed the perfect gentleman. In private, he was a monster.

"Papa is a viscount," she muttered but, if her mother heard her, the Viscountess Mortel did not respond.

1

*P*rudence was married for three months. Three months of torturous marriage was more than she could bear. As the mail coach bounced along the rutted roads she only hoped that she could get far enough away before the earl realized that she had left. If he found her, he would bring her back. If she stayed away, perhaps he could say she was dead. She might as well be dead.

Jasper Numbton, the Earl of Fondleton, was a monster and a rake. Prudence did her best to keep her features illegible of their torment. Not a tear or muffled sob would slip free. Years upon years of practice had taught the Baggington sisters to hide their woes. Prudence had thought marriage her salvation. Now, she carried nothing but a small carpet bag that rode in her lap as if it contained items too precious to be lashed to the top of the carriage.

"Halthaven ahead!" the driver called. The carriage

began to slow and Prudence felt her heart begin to thump in her chest anew.

She had taken a risk coming to Halthaven, a monumental risk. It would either be her deliverance or her undoing for if the earl discovered her escape she might never get the chance again. She was sure he would lock her away. His would be the only face she saw for the remainder of her days.

The other occupants climbed from the coach to stretch their legs but they would not be staying in the remote village. As soon as the horses were watered they would be on their way again, with no recollection of the quiet lady with her face shielded by a bonnet.

Alone in the coach Prudence struggled to pull the wedding band from her plump finger. It had been a source of protection during her journey but she had no need for it any longer. In fact, she wished nothing more than to forget that she had ever been married in the first place. With the ring's removal she felt somewhat lighter, more like herself, Prudence again rather than Lady Fondleton.

She slipped the plain metal ring into a velvet pouch and considered pushing it into the carpet bag, but decided it was best to leave it closed just now. It was best the contents of said bag remain secret. Instead, Prudence put the velvet pouch into her pocket and pushed the golden ring to the very bottom.

She wished she could forget about it entirely. She wished she could have left it behind, but of course, she could not. The ring was the only jewelry she carried. She had left the more costly ornaments at the manor. She did not wish to be accused of theft, even though as the countess the jewels were rightfully hers. She knew the earl did not love her, but if she took anything of value, Prudence knew he would hunt her down. She hoped that leaving empty handed would keep the earl from seeking her too vigorously.

Then, with as much pride as she could muster, she tucked her small bag close and descended the mail coach. She thanked the footman for handing her down. She had no coin for a tip except the one that was promised to the nuns, but she was grateful for his kindness. He smiled absently and looked away. For once, she was happy to know that her plain features would help her to be easily forgotten.

She had never been to Halthaven before, nor had she ever intended to visit. It was a shock to see the rush of activity in the isolated town. The arrival of the mail coach had spurred the excitement of the locals. Doors opened and slammed shut as patrons rushed to collect their letters or packages. An old woman with a cane and one milky blue eye watched Prudence with interest. Prudence turned her face away and held her bag close to her chest with two hands as she slipped down the street away from the crowd.

A sign swung and creaked in the wind, announcing a tavern named the Broken Bridle. Prudence was not sure of the level of clientele that would be housed within, nor did she care. The patrons could not be more repugnant than her own husband. She pushed her way into the dark and dank hall and made her way to the barkeep.

The burly man in a once white apron, polished the

glasses that sat in a row on the counter. His face was mostly covered with a surplus of facial hair. Both his hair and his beard looked like they could have used a trim weeks ago. He grinned at her, and she felt somewhat at ease by his ready smile.

"What can I help ya fer?" he grunted while replacing a glass and choosing another to shine. His eyes were on the glass.

Again, Prudence noted that she was not worth the lingering stares that would follow her sisters every time they showed their faces outside of the manor. Once again, she thanked God for her plain features.

She cleared her throat.

"If you would be so kind," she muttered hoarsely, cleared her throat again, and began anew. "If you would be so kind as to direct me toward Halthurst Abbey, I would be most grateful."

The man raised his gaze to look her over. Prudence stood under his appraisal from her bonnet to her toes with a nervous patience. Then, he gave one curt nod and turned his attention back to the glasses.

"Gon' be a nun, are ya?" he asked.

As a married woman Prudence would never be allowed to take such vows against those she had already stated, not while her husband lived, but there was no way for this man to know that. Rather, she would give whatever excuse might kept her identity concealed until she arrived at her destination.

"Yes, sir," she whispered. "I wish with all my heart that I would be worthy to dwell with the holy sisters." She lowered her head and did her best to give a modest and pious nod. Perhaps he often directed ladies toward the abbey. Prudence wondered if her own sister had stood here all those years ago and made the same request.

"You'll not get there any time soon," he revealed. "All this rain we've seen has got the throughway flooded. Bridge is washed out and no way across 'cept on foot."

"Oh," Prudence felt deflated. She turned to glance out of the window and saw that the sun was already well in the sky. "If I were to walk could I arrive by nightfall?" she asked.

The barkeep held one finger to the tip of his nose while he thought.

"Perhaps ya should wait 'til mornin,'" he offered.

"I'd rather not wait another moment, if it can be helped," she revealed. "If you think it can be done, please point me in the proper direction, and I shall go."

"I ought ter say no," he shrugged, "but ya look like a sturdy enough gal for it. Ya got a strong pair of boots on them feet of yours?"

Prudence shifted her feet beneath her gown. She was wearing her best walking boots in preparation for the journey but they were still made more for fashion than crossing the countryside. Another product of her London advice, she mused sadly.

"Of course," she lied. Prudence did not care if she had to climb barefoot up a mountainside if it meant getting to the abbey before darkness fell upon her. She was road weary and ready to be free of her burdens, if that were at all possible.

The man narrowed his eyes. For a moment she

worried that he might call her bluff, but it seemed that he decided to allow her to make her own bed, if she so wished it.

"Well," he nodded, "my daughters are brawny girls so I learned not ta expect less from a woman. It's not a trek for the weak but I see you'll not be swayed." He explained that she should follow the main road to the end of the village. Then, she should take the fork in the road to the left. Once she came to the bridge she'd have to find a more shallow place to ford, but the road led straight to the abbey if she just stayed upon it.

"Don' go to the right or you'll end up in the Baron's Wood," he warned. "It's mighty easy to get turned around in the woods. We might not find ya 'till Michaelmas since we've no way 'o knowin' if you didna get to the abbey, what with the road out and all."

She thanked the barkeep and offered him her last coin. The rugged man, who could scare the leather off a cow, let his shoulders droop as he looked upon her extended hand.

"Keep it, miss," he gave a soft grin. "If nothin' else, give it to the sisters up where you're goin'. They've done a world a good for this village. That's to be sure." Prudence realized that there was more heart in him than met the eye. She folded her hand back around the last coin to her name, tears welling in her eyes at such a simple kindness.

With a croaked word of thanks she left the tavern and made her way toward the edge of the village.

For a moment, she almost felt a hope that her faith might be renewed in humanity. Then, she recalled why she had found herself in the tavern in the first place, and she cursed the world of men, mostly her father and her husband. Then she bit her tongue and asked forgiveness. She should not go to the holy sisters with a curse in her mouth.

"If only you would take them both, Lord," she prayed. "I do not wish harm upon them, for that would be ungodly. I only wish they were in Your Presence rather than mine. I am too weak to suffer them."

2

*N*ight did fall before Prudence reached her destination. She had trudged along with a determination that she had not known she possessed, yet the time wasted finding a shallow place to cross the river had cost her precious hours.

She had removed her boots and stockings, tossed her skirts over her shoulder, and still not managed to climb up the opposing bank without leaving herself drenched from waist to toe. The added weight of her dresses slowed her to the point where she even considered walking for a mile or two in only her undergarments until her skirts dried. Her sensibilities would not allow it, so she placed her boots back upon her feet and dragged the sodden folds through the mud behind her.

When the light of the day began to fade she was thankful that the twinkle of candles in the windows of the abbey had come into view in the distance. That, and the ring of a bell that chimed every quarter of an hour kept her to the path, even when she was no longer certain that she was upon it.

Her stomach growled with the memory of her last meal, a bit of bread and cheese that had been stolen from the kitchens before her escape from her husband's home. The final morsel had been consumed shortly after she had begun to plod her way through the sodden trail away from the village. She prayed that the nuns might allow her a bite of something, anything, upon her arrival. The thought that she might have to wait until a communal morning meal made her groan in agony. Already, her head was beginning to ache and her stomach twisted and cried out.

Prudence was near delirium when she arrived at the steps of the abbey. She had been muttering nonsense into her bag for nigh on an hour, recalling the journey they had completed and how much better off life would be away from the earl.

"May I help you?" a soft voice startled Prudence from her reverie. She looked up into the soft, brown eyes of a frail looking nun who might have been the oldest person Prudence had ever laid eyes upon.

"Oh!" she gasped. "Umm... well..."

Now that she was here, she knew not what to say. She snapped her bag shut with a little squeak. She thought for a long while about the best way to begin. Rather than pry, the nun simply stood and waited with silent understanding.

All of a sudden, Prudence fell to her knees in supplication. "I pray you," she said.

"Pray to God," the nun said with a stern expression.

Prudence, still kneeling, clutched at the nun's grey habit. "Please, I've nowhere else to go," she cried. "I do not know what to do."

The nun's face softened as she bent down. "What is the matter my child?"

The old woman crouched at her side and pulled Prudence against her with surprising strength. Her fingers stroked Prudence's matted tresses and she cooed soft words of love and support. Prudence wished that she could stop the world in this moment and live in it forever.

She wiped the tears from her eyes and looked up into the face of her savior. The woman had clear blue eyes, and laugh lines about her lips, but the rest of her face was covered by her wimple.

"I don't know where to begin," Prudence whimpered.

"What led you here?" the old nun asked.

"My sister," Prudence said. "I hope she is here."

"Your sister?"

"Temperance!" Prudence exclaimed. The prospect of her sister being so near made Prudence want to rush into the abbey and call out for her sibling. "My sister," she explained. "I need to see my sister."

The old woman narrowed her eyes, taking in all that Prudence was and, perhaps, measuring her against her sister. Prudence hoped not for there was no comparison. Temperance was the most beautiful of the Baggington sisters. In fact, before she had abandoned Nettlefold for the abbey five years prior, Temperance had been the gem of the town.

"I see," was all that the nun said. She must have made some significant determination for she stood, set

Prudence upon her feet, and ushered her inside. After a moment, she spoke again. "I will speak with the Mother Abbess."

Prudence wondered what the Mother Abbess would do. Would she allow her to stay?

"May I take your things while you wait?" the nun said as she settled Prudence before a simple fire in a gaping hearth.

"No!" Prudence exclaimed and clutched the bag to her breast. Then, she recalled her manners and softened her tone. "Thank you," she amended. "I should like to keep it, if you don't mind."

"As you wish." The nun nodded and left the room on silent footsteps.

Prudence used the moment to evaluate her surroundings. She had been led into a bare room with little more than a writing desk and a pair of padded chairs. The walls were adorned with several paintings of the religious persuasion, but overall the room was bare.

Despite the empty expanse, it was not cold. In fact, she felt at once at home. If it would not have been rude, she might have curled up in the opposite chair and drifted off to sleep. Instead, due to the ruined nature of her gown, she chose a spindly wooden piece that was worn to the point of comfort from ages of use.

The door creaked open and another elderly, though not quite so old as the first, nun swept into the room with a grace that would befit The Queen.

"What is your name, child?" she asked as she settled herself at the writing desk.

"Prudence," she said after some hesitation.

"I am Sister Beatrice," the nun explained, "Mother Abbess of Halthurst Abbey. Your claim to be Temperance's sister would make you a Baggington, yet you have not identified yourself as such. What is your *proper* name?"

Prudence could see that, while the Mother Abbess seemed obliging enough at the moment, she would not put the question to her again.

"I am Lady Fondleton," she said with a heavy heart. "Wife to the Earl of Fondleton, Prudence Numbton, formerly Baggington."

"Thank you, Lady Fondleton," Sister Beatrice replied. She folded her hands upon her lap and looked upon Prudence with a firm expression. "The convent is no place for a married woman. Are you widowed?"

"N-no," Prudence stammered. It would not do to admit to a member of the holy order that she had very much prayed for just such a thing. "I am here to..."

"To see your sister," the Mother Abbess nodded. "Yes, I am aware."

"May I?"

"Temperance has some very important decisions to make." Sister Beatrice seemed disinclined to allow it and Prudence felt her hope sink into a puddle at her feet.

"I know that her decision to join your convent has meant that she should forsake her previous life," Prudence could think of no way to convince the nun other than to beg, "but I have come here for sanctuary. Even as a nun she is my sister, though you might not see it that way..."

"A nun?" Sister Beatrice raised one eyebrow. "When has your family last heard from Temperance?"

Prudence hung her head. "Not these past five years, since she left, though I cannot blame her." The admission broke her heart.

"Temperance has not yet joined our ranks," the Mother Abbess revealed.

"She hasn't?" Prudence was dumbfounded. Her sister had left home all those years ago with the vow that she would never marry, and never return. She would be a nun. She had sworn so. Though dozens of letters had been sent by all of the Baggingtons, Temperance had never responded. Prudence's heart sank. "Is... is she still here?"

"Oh yes," Sister Beatrice replied with a smile and a laugh at her visitor's clear relief. "She is a novice. Though it has taken her longer than most to take her vows, she has finally decided to make the ultimate commitment this coming spring. We are happy to have her as she has shown great promise these years in our care."

"Yes..." Prudence knew not what else to do other than agree.

"I suppose, as a novice, she might still receive a visit," Sister Beatrice gave a solemn nod. "Though, I hope that you do not intend to sway her from her determination to devote her life to The Lord."

"Not at all," Prudence promised. "I swear to you that I come here in my own need. I have no intention of uprooting Temperance or her devotions."

"We do not swear, Lady Fondleton," the Mother

Abbess replied, "but I thank you for the truth of your words."

Sister Beatrice slipped from the room and left Prudence once again to her silence. She did not know what to make of her reception. She had yet to be certain that she would be allowed to stay and every moment without that promise increased her fear.

"Prudence!" a delicate voice echoed in the hall. The patter of slippered feet could be heard rushing through the hall.

"Calm, my child," Sister Beatrice's cool voice came from behind.

"Yes, Mother," Prudence heard her sister reply along with the slowing of her footsteps.

Temperance Baggington, the eldest and most beautiful of all the daughters, stepped into the room with a perfectly contained posture and expression. Her beautiful hair was contained under her wimple. Prudence could not help but wonder if the nuns had cut it all off. Temperance's face was smooth and white, her lips pursed momentarily and then she broke into a smile, but that was the only indication that she was glad to see her sister. She kept herself still and sedate.

"Lady Fondleton," she said with a nod.

"Please do not call me that," Prudence said with a huff of laughter, perhaps bordering on hysteria.

"Is it true that you have been wed?" Temperance approached her sibling and grasped her hands within her own. Her eyes sparkled with the excitement of seeing her sister, but she maintained her composure for the pair of watchful eyes that entered the room a moment later. "I ought to offer you my congratulations."

Prudence knew not where to begin. She shook her head. "No. Do not congratulate me. There are no felicitations to be had," she informed her sister. Prudence threw a glance towards the nuns. How could she speak here? "My marriage is not what I had hoped," she explained.

"Most unions are not," Sister Beatrice replied.

"It is more than that." Prudence widened her brown eyes and implored her sister to understand the truth without words. She could not dare to make her confession in front of such a pure soul as the Mother Abbess. In fact, she dared not say a word to anyone if it could be helped.

"I beg you," she cried. "Do not send me back."

"Lady Fondleton," Sister Beatrice said with a sigh, "one cannot run from their responsibilities. A convent is not a place to hide from life."

Prudence dared not say that, in her opinion, it was exactly the place that one went with the desire to hide from life. That, of course, would get her nowhere. Instead, she remained silent and squeezed her sister's hands, begging Temperance to remember with her heart the language that they once shared.

"Remember Father," Prudence said.

Temperance's eyes widened and she tightened her grip on her sister's hands.

"If you might only give me a chance," Prudence begged. "I promise that I will not be a burden."

"The convent is no place for a married woman," the

Mother Abbess repeated. "We have no power to keep you here against your husband's will."

"He does not know where to find me," Prudence persisted.

Temperance loosed her hands from her sister and turned to the nun. "Reverend Mother," Temperance said in a soft murmur that she must have learned in her time at the abbey, "I beg you to reconsider. Prudence has never been one for dramatics. I assure you, if she is seeking safe haven it is within reason. At least, surely she must spend the night."

"Still," Sister Beatrice continued, "far be it from me to keep a gentleman, an earl no less, from his wife. The abbey is not meant to withstand such things. I am sure the earl's wrath would rain upon us. It is not within our power to hide you from him here."

"Please, Reverend Mother," Prudence said.

The Mother Abbess then turned to Prudence. "Is he a hateful man?" she asked.

"Hateful," Prudence thought on it for a long while. "I am not so certain that hateful is the word. He is a wolf in sheep's clothing, but a wolf is akin to a dog. He is more a monster." She spat bitterly.

Sister Beatrice nodded.

Prudence felt as if she could not express enough the danger that her husband presented. This nun could have no idea of his plotting or manipulations. Even worse, the sick nature of his mind.

"Jasper is different," Prudence said with grave sincerity. "He is unlike any other man, gentleman or no, that I have met. There is something... wrong about him."

"How long have you been married, child?" Sister Beatrice asked.

Prudence admitted to the few months which she had been formally wed. Still, it felt like an eternity.

"My child, I have had dozens of ladies come to my doors in shock at the changes of life after marriage," the nun explained. "Few are prepared for the truth of it. Ladies fill their heads with fairy tales and that is not what marriage is. Love is one thing, but reality is quite another."

"I assure you that I am not blinded by idealism," Prudence persisted.

"Still," the Mother Abbess continued, "we have no right to keep you here when you belong to another."

Her words brought about a finality that both Prudence and her sister knew better than to attempt to argue against. The Reverend Mother allowed that their guest might remain for the night only. In the morning, she would be returned to the village with express instruction to be delivered back to her husband.

3

*P*rudence could not fault the nun. She had a convent filled with women to look after and, while Prudence had hoped to hide amongst them, there was little that they could do to circumvent the will of an earl, or any gentleman of note for that matter. Still, she could not help but be crushed at the knowledge that her entire plan lay in pieces, a failure.

She thanked the nun for the offer of a bed and bath for the evening, declining the latter for sake of her own sanity.

"If you are to stay with us you will bathe, my lady," the Reverend Mother instructed. "Cleanliness is next to godliness."

"I am fine, I am sure," Prudence protested still clutching the bag close. "I would not want to inconvenience you."

The Mother Abbess gave her a look, and Prudence

was sure she thought Prudence did not want to bathe in such meager accommodations. That was not the case.

The old nun folded her arms over her ample breast. "Lady Fondleton, you may be more civilized than our usual ways, but you are worn by the road and I should expect a higher level of cleanliness during your stay within our walls. After your wash you shall also be fed, if you wish."

Prudence was not ashamed by the lecture. She was not one who was used to such a slovenly state. Yet, neither did she wish to bathe in the presence of these women of faith, for she had been offered the aid of their hands despite her assurance that she could manage on her own. The temptation of a meal was the only thing that allowed her mind to be swayed.

Temperance linked her arm through her sister's and steered her down the hall and toward the bathhouse.

"Really," Prudence muttered, "I am leaving in the morning, I shall not need a wash."

Temperance shook her head at her sister as she had used to when they were children. The shine of her deep brown eyes glinted in the candlelight.

"Prudence, you ought to bathe," she whispered. "You are waist deep in mud and leaving a trail with each step. We shall clean for a month after your visit."

Prudence glanced behind her where there was, in fact, a trail of crumbling dirt in her wake. With a sigh of resignation she agreed to the task. At least the nuns would be civil about it, she thought. At the very least they knew how to keep their own council, unlike most ladies' maids.

Her gown was stripped and hastened off to be cleaned as best as was possible. If there was any chance of saving the dress, it would be attempted, though Prudence thought it might be best to just cut it to rags at this point.

Temperance and one other postulant were given the task of assisting their guest with the bath. A lowly job, Prudence realized, for the others were surely fast asleep in their beds at this hour.

Prudence was surprised when her sister remained silent.

"Really Prudence, what were you thinking?" were the scolding words that she had expected to hear from her sister's mouth. Instead, Temperance set about her task with singular focus. Five years cloistered and she had seemed to forget how to speak.

"Temperance." Prudence put her hand upon her sister's arm as she reached out to untie her undergarments. The other postulant, a freckle-faced girl with brassy hair and eyes that were set wide in her face, never gave her name as she hauled buckets of boiled water into the basin.

Temperance looked into her sister's eyes, resigned to their fates. There was nothing more that could be done now that the Abbess had made her decision.

Prudence released a deep sigh and turned her back to allow her sister better ease in the task. She felt fingers at the laces upon her back.

Then, a gasp.

Cool air hit Prudence's back as the sheath slipped from her shoulders and down along the winding curves of her body. What had once been peaks and valleys of pale, milky skin was now mottled with purples and greens. The sickly pallor of bruises newly acquired beside those in the later stages of healing brought both postulants to her side.

Soft fingers traced the ridges of her back, puckered welts from where she had been beaten with a strap. Ligature marks from restraints marked her limbs, a telltale sign of the earl's preferences.

A soft plea to The Lord was whispered as trembling fingers traced the tender flesh that was scarred and scabbed in several places. There was the distinct shape of a human bite mark. Hidden beneath the fabric of her gown, Prudence's body was a graveyard of violent memory.

Nary an inch was left unmarred save that which might be exposed to public view. Jasper Numbton was practiced enough to keep his violent perversions masked to the outside world. Rather, his wife had been left to suffer in silence as she learned to hide the marks and bear through the pain of his assaults.

Not a word needed to be said to send the other postulant racing from the room in terror.

"It's alright," Temperance murmured as she wrapped her arms around her sister's naked frame. "He cannot hurt you any longer, little sister. I promise you that."

Prudence did her best not to shrink away from Temperance's protective embrace. The kindness of human touch had been forgotten for such a long time that it was all that she could do not to flinch as the gentle hands guided her into the warm waters.

"There is nothing that can be done," Prudence sobbed as tears began to stream into the bath. "if the sisters won't let me stay, where will I go?"

"There must be a way," her sister said with a vigor that seemed to spring forth from some forgotten reservoir.

"I am wed," Prudence whispered in her meek voice a mantra she had been taught to repeat in recent months. "I *belong* to him."

"You belong to God," Temperance spat.

"No," Prudence said. "God has forsaken me."

"Blasphemy," Temperance said. "A gentleman of this ilk has no right to a wife."

"You say that," Prudence protested, though the word of support was like a balm to her wounds, "but you forget what the world is like outside of these walls. Men are unkind. Have you forgotten?"

Temperance's eyes grew dark, almost black with anger that seethed just beneath the surface.

"I have never forgotten," she asserted. "Nor will I." Her voice was low, dangerous, and certainly nothing that might come to be expected from one who was soon to take her vows of poverty, chastity, faith, and charity. For a moment, Prudence glimpsed the spark that she had once known her sister to possess. That is, before it was covered with the demure focus of one who was to wash every speck of dirt from her sister's exhausted limbs.

They continued in silence, the practice of sisterly conversation having been forgotten in their isolations.

When the door opened once more, Prudence expected the figure that entered to be that of the mute postulant. Instead, it was none other than the Mother Abbess herself.

"Stand, my child," she instructed with a soft wave of her hand as if she might compel Prudence from the waters.

Instinct forced her to shrink down into the warmth so that the suds that floated along the surface of the bath masked the flaws of her flesh.

"I must see for myself." The Reverend Mother allowed an expression of pain to cross her features, revealing that she hoped that what she had been told was not true, or perhaps an exaggeration.

Prudence glanced at her sister, still kneeling beside the basin. Temperance nodded in silence.

With her breath held tight in her chest and her eyes cast downward, Prudence rose from the water to reveal the freshly cleaned surface of her skin.

It was worse than the Mother Abbess had anticipated, there could be no mistake about that. Now that the mud had been washed away, several more bite marks had become apparent. Areas that had merely looked unclean, were now unmistakably an extension of the pattern of bruises that trailed across her body.

The Mother Abbess's hand flew to her mouth, and when she took it from her lips she spoke in a soft voice. "The church demands a wife submit to her husband, but this..." She shook her head. "I do not believe The Lord requires a wife to submit to torture." She waved Prudence back to the cooling water. "You will stay here as long as necessary until I might find a safe place to hide you away," she promised.

Prudence felt as if she could cry anew, but there were no tears left in her. Instead, she sank down in shocked silence at the turn of events in her favor.

"It is well that the road is out for it shall prevent visitors, and questions," the nun continued. "That shall purchase us a few days' time to form a plan."

Prudence was peppered with questions about her husband and the likelihood that he might pursue her. Without a doubt, Prudence confirmed their worst fears.

"He is a proud man and likes nothing more than a challenge," she admitted. "In fact, I am not entirely certain that he would not take great personal pleasure in... the hunt."

She shivered at the realization that she was now little more than prey in his game. Lord Fondleton would come after her with his full effort. No expense would be spared. She had hoped that leaving the jewels would satisfy him, but she knew that was not so. He would not rest until he had won. She wondered if there was anywhere that might be safe. Perhaps even the colonies would not be too far for his extensive reach.

"There is one more thing..." Prudence grimaced as she stepped from the water and pulled a long length of cloth around herself for both coverage and absorption.

"Are you with child?" the Mother Abbess asked with wide, fearful eyes.

"Not that I am aware of," Prudence shook her head.

She could see the relief in the eyes of the other two women. A child would present another layer of complications. She might be able to run from him, but he would not allow his heir to be taken. Just to be safe, she sent a plea to the heavens that her womb remained untouched. Her husband had seemed to be more intent on other pleasures than the act which might get her with child.

"Just one more thing..." she said again.

"Then, out with it," the nun pressed. "We haven't all night."

Prudence pressed her lips together in a nervous gesture that prevented her from groaning at her plight. She had only barely been accepted into the abbey, and only for the state of her health. There was no guarantee that they would be forgiving of any further surprises.

She padded over to her carpet bag, which sat in the corner. The sound of her damp feet upon the cool stone floor was all that could be heard. She would have to get used to the silent nature of these women. The bag had been left open, but she pulled the mouth wider to peer inside. A small yip greeted her.

"You're awake!" she whispered, her face transforming into a wide grin.

"You said there was no child!" Sister Beatrice exclaimed. "What have you done?" It was clear that she thought Prudence had stolen a child and carried it in her bag. The truth was not so far from her assumption.

She reached into the recesses of the nearly empty container. She had packed no other clothing save the dress she wore. Those that she possessed would have drawn too much attention. Besides, she thought, she hated them all.

Instead, she had brought only herself. She still felt a twinge of regret at the loss of her mother's comb, but knew that her mother would forgive the haste of her escape.

Her hands cradled the tiny life within and she drew it from the darkness and held it against her breast. There, it curled against the cloth that covered her body, opened its mouth into a wide yawn, and settled against her.

"Why, it is a puppy!" Temperance exclaimed and rushed to her sister's side to peer at the small creature.

"Whatever made you bring that creature with you?" Sister Beatrice asked, though it was clear from her tone that she had a heart that was fond of animals. Prudence held the small brown pup, as plain as herself, out to the nun who took it with a small gasp and a sigh.

"She was the runt," Prudence explained. "Jasper was going to have her drowned. I heard him speak of it. I couldn't leave her, I just couldn't bear the thought. We both escaped. Together."

Sister Beatrice looked indignant at the prospect of the loss of life.

"I shouldn't allow it," she murmured while her fingers stroked the feather-soft fur of the animal's ears. "Really, it's a luxury... an extra mouth to feed."

"She's too small to cause any issues," Temperance reasoned. "Really, I doubt she can do more than hobble at this point. A rag of milk will fill her belly. That is not too much to spare. I'll even forego my own glass if you'd like, Mother."

Sister Beatrice was humming to the waking pup as she rocked back and forth. A tiny, pink tongue flicked out and tasted her hand. Her heart melted before Prudence's eyes.

"I shall have to find a place that can take you both," Sister Beatrice concluded. "It shall be your duty to keep her care. I'll not have a spectacle in my abbey."

"Of course," Prudence could not keep the grin from her face. It appeared that they had both been saved this night, she and Posey, as she had come to call the pup during her trek to the abbey.

She had let the animal down from her bag as she sat for a moment to rest her blistered feet. The small brown puppy had done its best to waddle through the field of flowers that bordered the lane, attacking each small flower with a vengeance that was contrary to her minuscule size. Prudence had laughed at the battle between the pup and its namesake. Posey, she had decided would be her name.

Sister Beatrice made her farewells so that she might compose a letter to be delivered by the groundskeeper that very evening. The cover of darkness would prevent any suspicions while also allowing her to act with utmost urgency. Prudence wondered to whom she might be writing and how they might come to her aid.

Temperance assisted her in dressing. The rough woolen gowns that the postulants wore were nothing more than a sheath compared to her usual gowns. Still, she did not complain. She would disguise herself as a shrub if that was what it took to evade Lord Fondleton.

The offer of sustenance for herself and the pup was accepted with gratitude. Temperance procured a small hunk of bread and butter along with a bowl of some sort of mash that Posey gobbled up without hesitation. Prudence was proud to witness her growth and knew that it was only a matter of time before the dog was as healthy as any.

Prudence was weary and relieved for the offer of a small room with a sleeping mat in the corner and a pile of warm blankets to crawl beneath. She wanted to ask her sister to stay with her, to rest at her side as they had when they needed to guard against the terrors of the night as children, but Temperance had murmured her farewell and slipped away into the dormitory where she would be expected to sleep amongst her peers.

It still hurt Prudence to think that her sister was to be so removed from their family. Yet, she could not blame her. Temperance had received the brunt of the burden that the Baggington sisters had to endure as a result of her pure and extraordinary beauty.

Prudence had always thought it amusing that the gossips of Nettlefold proper referred to herself, and her family, as *the baggage.* It was true that they carried a surplus of secrets indeed, she had often thought. Only, the mental rather than physical sort. Little did the gossips know just how many secrets their family concealed in the isolation of the cold manor walls.

Prudence fell to sleep that evening without a nightmare. It was the first time in months that her mind had drifted into the relief of blackness. She cared not if she slept until lunchtime. She cared not if she did not even wake at all.

4

Prudence spent the next two days hidden away in the tiny room with nothing more than Posey and a small circular window with a view of the clouds to occupy her time. Temperance returned twice a day with a small tray of plain food, a crust of bread with a bowl of soup or a boiled egg and an apple, but she dared not stay too long to converse.

Posey was well fed and loved, though she did tear the feathers from a pillow one evening. The eldest Baggington once brought a Bible for her sister to read but it lay abandoned on the widowsill. How could she read the Bible when she had abandoned her husband? Prudence would not have minded a frivolous novella or compilation of poetry, but of course the nuns would never possess such items.

Sister Beatrice was right to keep her hidden away from the others. There were nearly seventy women that resided within the convent's protective walls. Far too many to risk a word slipping out of her arrival. The few that had met Prudence that fateful evening had been sworn to secrecy.

It was not until the fifth day that the isolation began to feel oppressive. Prior to that it was like a haven of silence and peace. Now, she wished to feel a breeze upon her face or hear the sound of another's voice. Perhaps it was that her body was finally able to begin its process of healing. Her bruises were fading, though some would take longer to disappear in their entirety. The welts had lessened with the help of small poultices and rubs that had been provided and even her muscles were beginning to move without aches and the sharp stabs of pain that had become commonplace.

Though she would always sport a series of scars, forever marked by the devilish grasp of her husband, Prudence cared not. So long as she was free of him, she could breathe. Besides, like her sister, she was determined never to trust the touch of a man again. A lesson Prudence had now learned twice over. She wished that she could still hope, at least for the sake of her brothers, that some men might not be so unkind. They, at least, had never shown sign of brutality or malice. Though, Prudence sighed, they still had many years in which to learn the trait that seemed, in her mind, to lay dormant within all of the men of the world.

WHEN THE DAY ARRIVED THAT PRUDENCE WAS CALLED from her isolation and into the meeting chamber of the

Mother Abbess, she could not suppress her nerves. Perhaps Lord Fondleton had already found her. Had the abbey been forced to hand her over? Or would she be told that there was no help to be had and forced out onto the street like a thief or vagrant?

Oh, how she wished that she could have carried Posey with her for support. Instead, the pup remained behind in the care of the red haired postulant, whose face broke into a cheerful grin as she coddled the animal and offered it a small treat.

Temperance linked her arm through her sister's.

"What is to become of me?" Prudence asked.

"Sister Beatrice has been writing letters nonstop for days," Temperance revealed. "I do not know yet what she has planned, but I am certain that she will have done all in her power to protect you."

"Are you certain?" Prudence asked with a hitch in her voice. "Mightn't she turn me over to his Lordship and wash her hands of me?"

Temperance shook her head and offered a solemn consolation. "Sister Beatrice is a kindred spirit," she revealed. "She has been most patient with my..." Temperance shook her head as if to clear it. "Let us just say that she is far more understanding than she lets on."

"She knows... everything?" Prudence asked with wide eyes.

"I'm afraid so," Temperance confirmed. "Not at first, I'll admit, but over the years I have grown to trust her and she has been patient with me in my times of need."

Prudence nodded but it did not quell the fear in her heart. She felt as if she were approaching the gallows to face her judgement. Her whole future hinged upon this moment. She felt ill.

"A breath, love," Temperance instructed. It had been many years since she had been the protector of the Baggington daughters. Prudence had missed her sister's strength and firm resolve. She wished that she could bottle it and carry it with her forever. Prudence had never had the confidence to stand tall, when she had always felt so much less than those around her. Temperance, on the other hand, had an iron firm will that refused to be broken.

As a child, she had spent years jealous of every detail of Temperance's face. Her tall, lean frame had been coveted. It was only when they had reached the years prior to coming of age that Prudence had understood what a burden beauty could be. Their father's lustful stares and lingering fingers had taken years to drive Temperance away as she had attempted, and failed, to protect her sisters from his grasp. It was only the week before her first season that she had finally taken flight. Neither Prudence, nor the others, could blame her.

It made Prudence sick to think that she had once been jealous of their father's preference. Of course, she had not yet witnessed his depravity at that time. By the time her eyes had been opened to the truth of it all, it was too late. Temperance had fled and the Viscount Mortel had been enraged as never before. Soon, the prospect of marriage, and freedom, was all that his daughters could think of. His wife, below his interest in her old age, had focused all her energies on the task.

"Enter," the cool voice of Sister Beatrice called from within.

The sisters stepped through the doorway and allowed the heavy oak panel to swing shut behind them. Seated at her writing table was the Mother Abbess. Her rod straight back and immovable features seemed in contrast to the gentleman who leaned with one arm against the hearth as if bored to have been called here.

"Please, sit," the nun instructed.

Prudence waited for the light to spark in his eyes as Temperance stepped into view. To her everlasting surprise, it did not. She wondered if he were so used to the chaste nature of the women within the abbey that he did not even truly see them.

Good, she thought. Perhaps she might blend in as intended. Not, she reminded herself, that she had ever stood out to anyone.

The sisters sat but the gentleman remained at the hearth.

"George," Sister Beatrice began, "how is Marietta?"

Prudence was surprised that she was so familiar as to refer to him by his Christian name.

"As well as can be expected," he replied with a shrug.

"As I thought from her letters," the nun replied, nodding. "Now, George, I am in need of your services. Or rather, I wish for you to formally request mine. It should appear that you sought our help at the abbey, if you would."

The gentleman's face broke into a grin. He was amused and not at all surprised by her request. Prudence wondered how often he was called upon to perform secretive services for the Abbess.

"What this time, Aunt?" he said with a laugh.

"Marietta is in need of a companion, is she not?" The Reverend Mother continued without pause. "I would like you to take Prudence, here, under your protection for Marietta's comfort." The nun gestured at Prudence, whose eyes were still wide at the thought of being introduced with only her Christian name. However, she knew she certainly could not go by Lady Fondleton. An elbow to her ribs from Temperance closed her mouth and had her offering a shy smile.

"Is she a real postulant?" the gentleman asked with disbelief.

"She is something of the sort," the Reverend Mother replied.

"What am I to do with her?" he asked with a sigh of resignation.

"The same as usual," the Reverend Mother offered with a shrug. "Ensure that she cannot be found."

Rather than responding, the man took his hat from the ledge and shoved it down atop his head. Sister Beatrice seemed to take that as a sign of assent for she turned to the sisters and clapped her hands together as if the matter was resolved.

"Prudence, this is my nephew, the Baron Halthaven." Sister Beatrice made the introductions. "He shall offer you our family home and protections until I can manage a more suitable, and distant, arrangement." She gave a knowing glance to the sisters, "I assure you that he has impeccable honor and character. No harm shall befall you if it is within his means to prevent. Does this suit you?"

"Oh yes," Prudence clasped her hands in relief. "Thank you, ever so much Reverend Mother, and you as well, Lord Halthaven." Two nods returned her kindness.

"Now," the Mother Abbess continued, "I expect you shall behave as a postulant of our order. Novice Temperance will be sent to check on you when we can spare her duties. Otherwise, it would be best that you kept to yourself and the grounds of Halthaven."

"Thank you, Reverend Mother," Prudence repeated, deeply grateful. She did not care where the baron lived, nor how wealthy or lowly he might be. If only she could find some safe corner of the countryside while she awaited a more permanent chance to escape her husband.

She would provide companionship for his wife, or sister, or daughter, whomever Marietta might be. On second thought, she determined, the baron seemed far too young to have a daughter of such age as to need companionship. He was, at most, only a year or two her senior. She decided that Marietta was likely a wife or sister, perhaps ill and withdrawn to the country. Either way, Prudence did not care. Hope bloomed within her for the first time in months. Within the next ten minutes the carriage was called and her bag had been gathered and set upon the rack.

"No!" Prudence cried out, worried that Posey might be hidden in the carpet bag once again.

"Not to worry, Miss," the brassy haired postulant appeared with the sleeping Posey cradled in her arms. A yellow ribbon had been tied about the pup's neck and she looked well fed.

"What is this?" Baron Halthaven asked good-naturedly. He seemed immune to his aunt's surprises and never rattled by them.

"This is Posey," Prudence said with a grimace. "Do you mind?"

"Do I have a choice?" he laughed. "I am sure my aunt would have a word or two for my ear if I abandoned the beast on her step."

"I suppose you ought to leave us both," Prudence said before she could stop herself. The weakness of her spirit often burst forth when she was nervous. Why should this gentleman have any reason to help her?

"I should never defy the Reverend Mother," he replied. "I should have a convent full of nuns calling the plagues down upon me." He pretended to shiver as if afraid of their divine power.

Prudence felt a short burst of laughter creep forth before she stifled it. With a muffled apology, she bowed her head and did her best to remain silent. Jasper had not permitted any sign of happiness in his house. If she seemed to relax for a moment, he renewed his abuse with increased force as if to prove that he could break her of mirth.

The Baron Halthaven narrowed his eyes, as if he wished to comment upon her reaction but he stayed his tongue.

"My aunt seems to have been remiss in her introductions," he said instead. "I should be honored to offer you my protection, Miss...?" He left the name hanging as a question.

Prudence knew the Reverend Mother had neglected her surname on purpose. A nun could not lie after all. Still she would never again willingly say she was Lady Fondleton, nor Mrs. Numbton. Still she knew she could not use her maiden name of Baggington either. She was not yet far enough away that word of her whereabouts may not reach Lord Fondleton.

"Riverford." Prudence lied quickly, thinking of the river she had crossed on her way to the abbey. She was determined to leave all the hurts of the past on the far bank.

After a brief farewell, a lingering embrace with her sister, and a basket of the abbey's renowned bread to convey to the baron's cook, they were on their way. The carriage bumped along the road behind the convent and it was not until nearly a quarter hour had passed that Prudence recalled that the rain had damaged the route from the village. With her head craned toward the window, she peered out to see trees, rather than fields passing by.

"What is this lane?" she asked as they headed further into the wood.

"It is a service road that connects with my estate," he explained. "With the collapse of the bridge it is the only way to bring a carriage to Halthurst Abbey."

"Do the townsfolk know of it?" she asked. She recalled that the barkeep had thought there no access to the abbey by any route save foot.

"Not well," he explained. "I employ very few servants,

most of whom have been with the family for generations. They are very loyal. Halthaven is a private estate. This road is only used to make deliveries to the abbey after the harvests or in times of need. There is no access save through my properties."

"I see," she mused. For the first time Prudence allowed herself to evaluate the gentleman who sat on the opposite bench. He had chestnut hair with a curl above the ears as if he had forgotten to have it trimmed. His eyes were dark, though in the light of the carriage she could not be certain of their color except that it was in the range of earthen tones. The angles of his face were soft and though he was taller than Prudence she did not find his appearance as imposing or terrifying as many of the gentlemen that she was known to encounter. He was attractive enough, but there was nothing beastly about him.

At least, not in the physical sense, she thought to herself. Her husband had taught her well enough that it was a sickness of the mind that made a forceful man, more than the strength of his body. Still, Prudence found herself at ease with the Baron Halthaven's countenance. He seemed relaxed, non-threatening and unassuming in his manner.

She allowed a moment to pass into silence, not wishing to reveal too much of herself that might cause suspicion. Posey lay curled in her lap as they bumped along and she scratched the pup behind its ears whenever she stirred.

"You do not have many things," the baron stated after some time.

"No," she confirmed. "I had not thought to need them at the abbey." Nor had she wished for the memory of her previous life. Her fanciful belongings did not suit her. She had known that for years and had still given in to her mother's ploy. Now, she wished to be free of every negative memory that she could recall. She wished to be a different person than before. This was a chance for a fresh beginning. This was the chance to make herself anew and to be the person that she had always been inside. She would give up all wealth and titles if it only meant that she could escape her past. Prudence would much prefer a common life to life as Lady Fondleton.

"Then," he wondered, "you had wished to stay?"

She knew that she was willfully misunderstanding his words when she replied. He had thought she wished to be a postulant, though with unfinished business or danger to attend before vows could be made. The reality was that she would never be fit to be a nun, especially not in her married state. Still, it was easier to allow him to believe her devoted to the order than to explain the mess that she had found herself. He was a peer, she recalled. Though the lower form than an earl he still might harbor some loyalty to the others of his class. She could not risk that the baron might hand her over to Lord Fondleton.

"That would have been ideal," she agreed.

"Might I ask from what is it that you run?"

Prudence bristled at the question. Lord Halthaven seemed to sense her discomfort, for he waved away her requirement for a response.

"I only meant that my aunt has sent several postulants to bide their time at my estate." He explained that some would await the birth of a child to be adopted before their commitment, or seek forgiveness in the church from legal repercussions of a deviant life, or even the avoidance of impending nuptials for an unwanted marriage arrangement. "Never has she spoken of arranging even further sanctuary. I only wondered what the difference might be in your case."

"I am grateful for your assistance," Prudence replied. "Please, do not doubt that. However, my path is my own and I have been instructed to keep my silence."

"Of course," he replied. "I shall not ask again. I only hope that you understand that Marietta is very dear to me and I should not wish her to be... influenced... in any way unbefitting of a lady."

Prudence sighed. Of course the baron would be worried for the lady in his care. For all he was aware he was bringing some criminal to be her companion.

"I assure you that I am well aware of my duties." Prudence placed her hand above her heart to express her pure intention. For the first time in years her ample bosom was covered to the neck in fabric and she did her best to contain her amusement at the fact that her motion had done nothing to draw a gaze of masculine appreciation.

The baron looked only at her face with honest interest. For the first time, Prudence felt as though she were an equal.

"Your wife will not be compromised in any way," she promised. "I pose no threat of improper behavior. You have my word."

"Marietta is not my wife," the Baron Halthaven

revealed with an amused quirk of his brow. Prudence found the look appealing but then squashed the thought for although not truly a postulant she had vowed to forsake the male sex for all ages.

"I apologize for the assumption," she replied.

"It is no matter," he laughed. "I only thought you should know that she is young and will take much amusement."

"Is that so?" she asked. "A young sister, perhaps?"

"Neither," he shook his head and turned to acknowledge that they had reached the edge of the estate. "She is my charge. The orphaned daughter of my cousin. He died in the war and left her to my care."

"Might I ask her age?"

"She is two and ten, next summer," he revealed.

Prudence was glad that his gaze was elsewhere for her cheeks grew hot at the number. Two and ten was the year that Prudence had first heard the door to her chamber creep open in the night. It was the first time she had been looked upon as anything more than a child. It was the year that every dream in her world had been shattered.

She clamped her teeth together. She knew not a thing about this young Miss Marietta but she swore that with every breath within her no man would touch that child's innocent form. Her gaze settled upon the baron and she wondered if he had the gall to take advantage of his charge. Many a gentleman did. It was well known that a lord might wed his charge if she pleased him. The thought made Prudence sick to her stomach.

No, she reminded herself. Temperance had said that the Abbess knew well of the Baggington secrets. The

Reverend Mother was this man's aunt. She had spoken to his character. She would not place Prudence in the hands of a molester. The Baron Halthaven was safe.

Prudence considered that she need not fear this gentleman. She only needed protect the young lady from any other who might take liberties. Prudence knew more than most how common that type could be.

She remained silent for the remainder of the journey through the wood. If this child had the chance at a decent life, Prudence would do everything within her power to ensure it. As the wheels rolled on she sent a silent prayer up to the heavens.

Keep Jasper away from this place and all those who live here. May he never set foot upon this beautiful land and may he never again harm another living soul.

She dared not wish for his death, for that would be a sin, but a small part of her prayed that he would simply go away. Only then, might the world, and Prudence, be free of his control.

5

*P*rudence had not been aware that she had drifted off to sleep until a hand upon her arm woke her from her dream. She gasped awake twisting away, turning her face to her shoulder to guard against an attack.

The jolt of her body dislodged sweet Posey, who tumbled off of the lady's lap and onto the floor of the carriage.

A deep voice murmured a soft apology as a shadow bent down to scoop up the scampering pup. It took Prudence a moment to recall where she was, and with whom. She was glad for the drawn curtains of the carriage for there was no doubt that her ivory skin had deepened into a crimson blush. Her heart raced and she had yet to find her words. To her everlasting relief, she was not forced to speak or even acknowledge her reaction.

"We will arrive any moment," Lord Halthaven

informed her with a voice as calm and cool as if he had not taken note of her jitters. She appreciated his discretion. Prudence reminded herself that she would have to do better at masking her fears if she were to pull off this farce. Still, having been awakened many a night to the terrors of the darkness meant that she usually did well to ensure that she never drifted to sleep under the eye of a witness. Her waking hours were well controlled. Her sleep gave free rein to nightmares.

"Thank you," she whispered with her face turned down into her lap. She set about the task of adjusting her skirt. The heavy fabric was crumpled and folded like a vice around her legs from the carriage ride. When Prudence felt that she had composed herself into a decent state, she looked up to her companion to see him attempting to tug his shirtsleeve from the sharp grasp of the playful pup. Posey released a halfhearted growl and shook her head with a vigor that resulted in a tear in his fine linen shirt.

Prudence gasped and began spouting her apologies. She reached for the animal and did her best to free the gentleman from his attacker without further damage to his person. The pup was lively after her long rest and wanted nothing more than to continue her romp. She wiggled free of Prudence's grasp and slid across the floor of the carriage to clamp her teeth around the leather laces of the gentleman's boot.

"Oh dear," Prudence exclaimed. Her eyes searched the gentleman's face but found no hint of anger. Rather, he seemed amused by the feisty creature that was determined to make her mark. "Perhaps it might be mended?" she wondered.

Lord Halthaven inspected his cuff and deemed it reparable. He made the statement as if it were no matter. Prudence could not help but sigh with relief as he once more scooped up the puppy and handed it back to its owner. She wondered if he had an immense reserve of patience or was merely a skilled actor. Perhaps, she thought, he would fly into a rage when he thought no one was looking. Prudence could name but a handful of men that she suspected to be above fits of temper. Even those, she thought, might still possess the demon when out of the sight of gentle folk.

She stroked Posey until the animal was settled. The small, willful eyes were still alert and mischievous. Prudence made a mental note that she must be better at keeping her from trouble, and from wrestling with the baron's wardrobe.

The memory brought a small smile to her face and she was forced to press her lips together to conceal it. As the carriage began to slow, Prudence pulled back the curtain to peer at the elegant estate that lay ahead. The buildings were of middling size. Certainly nothing to be ashamed of, she thought, but not so grand as some of those that she had visited back in Nettlefold. Despite its modest stature, every inch of the land and buildings was maintained to perfection. Prudence could tell at once that the home was well loved by both its master and those under his employ.

A row of rosebushes lined the stone drive. Now that the summer was ended, they were bare save for the well-manicured greenery. She closed her eyes and attempted to imagine their beauty when covered with the wide blooms of red or white blossoms. Perhaps they might even be a rarer breed of pale pink.

She could almost smell them in her mind, as the carriage rolled down the lane. How wonderful it must be to be here in the summer. She felt a moment of sadness that she would never see such a sight. Here she was with the autumn upon her and the prospect of leaving at any moment. Beautiful or not, she would never see the rosy lane in the summer.

She was thankful that the Reverend Mother would go to such lengths to secure her safekeeping. Prudence only wondered how far she might have to travel to procure it. Perhaps she would be sent away to some land of perpetual ice where roses never bloomed and summer never came. Or perhaps the savagery of the colonies. She tried to be disappointed at the thought but even that was preferable to the threat of Lord Fondleton.

The steward and the housekeeper were waiting upon the step when the carriage rolled to a stop. Solemn nods and kind eyes revealed that they too were familiar with the nature of the gentleman's guests. Prudence was handed down from the carriage by the footman, who passed her sole piece of luggage to the housekeeper.

The woman was rail-thin with a sharp jawline and wisps of grey curls that sprung out from the edges of her cap. Prudence liked her at once. She seemed the sort of no-nonsense female that would not ask questions or pry while still able to keep strict control over the house and all those that resided within.

"Mr. Perkins," Lord Halthaven introduced the steward, "and his wife will see to your every need. Do not hesitate to seek their service."

Prudence nodded.

She could not imagine the couple paired as husband and wife. Mr. Perkins was a giant of a man. His wife could easily be tucked beneath his arm, like a mother hen might hide a chick. He seemed more suited as a stable master, she thought, due to his sheer strength and size. That is, until she saw him move. For a beast of a man he was surprisingly graceful. On silent steps he opened the door and swept the group into the entryway. As if from midair he procured a silver platter, upon which were the day's correspondence for the baron as well as a mouthful of wine each to refresh the travelers from their short, albeit rugged, journey.

"If you'll follow me, Miss," Mrs. Perkins said as she turned her back and began to walk down the hall. She expected to be followed without question, but Prudence was unsure. Lord Fondleton had allowed no female to speak before him, or give orders within his home. For that reason alone he had difficulty keeping a housekeeper and proper maids. Instead, he had resorted to bribery and threats to keep those who worked within the walls of his estate loyal and quiet.

Prudence deferred to the lord of the house for permission with a questioning look. He nodded and continued his conversation with the steward about matters of estate that were in need of attention. Prudence considered herself dismissed and followed after the housekeeper with Posey scrambling to release herself and explore the new location.

"You ought to change into something more comfortable," Mrs. Perkins said as she pulled a ring of keys from the folds of her gown and unlocked the door to the quaint chamber in which Prudence was to stay. "This'll be your room," she said. "Here's a key, not that you'll need it but it's yours if you'd like."

Prudence grasped the key as if it contained life itself. Such a luxury as a lock she had never been allowed. Now, the offer was almost more than she could bear. She held back a battering of tears, the Baggington refusal to show weakness still ingrained in her very soul.

"I'll have your other bags brought up if you would like to freshen up before meeting the young Miss." With a clap of her hands a young boy appeared to fulfill her request.

"I have nothing else," Prudence explained with a blush. Never in her life had she wanted for anything that a lady might need to keep up appearances. Even in all of his horror, Jasper had spared no expense on the appearance of showering his wife with finery. Just as her father had done, Lord Fondleton knew that the appearance of wealth and comfort was enough to stave off even the most observant of eyes.

"No?" Mrs. Perkins asked. "A true postulant then, are you?"

It seemed that all those within the protection of the estate were aware of the precarious nature of the young ladies that came to stay on occasion. Rather than make a fuss, she instructed the boy to take the puppy to the stables where she could be fed and allowed to romp as puppies were known to do.

"Well then," The housekeeper continued before Prudence was forced to formulate an answer, "I suppose we ought to have some fabrics sent up from the village."

"Please, no!" Prudence cried. She did not wish to be a burden upon the Lord Halthaven who had already gone so far as to grant her safe shelter. Besides, she thought, The Reverend Mother had given her firm instruction to remain beneath the notice of the villagers. The last thing that Prudence needed was suspicion of her presence floating around town.

"What I mean is," she clarified, "I do not expect to be here for long. I do have the gown I arrived in. It will need some patching but I can manage if you'll be so kind as to offer me some scraps and a needle."

"Nonsense," Mrs. Perkins opened the bag and pulled her ruined travel gown from its depths. The nuns had been unable to salvage the fabric, which was torn and tattered from the height of her knees and on down. "I shall have Lizzie fix it up nice enough," she said with a nod. "She has a fine hand with the needle and is fast as a whip."

"I shouldn't wish to put her out," Prudence protested.

"She's begging for a task," Mrs. Perkins said with an exaggerated sigh. "My daughter is fit to burst with those babies she's carrying. Bless her heart. Doctor says it's a pair! He bound her to the bed this last month to keep the labor from coming on early and she has been feisty as broke-hoofed burro with nothing to do but read. She'll mend your dress up right as rain. I even think we could take in a few of her gowns, if you'd like. She's a bit wider about the waist at the moment but the bust should fit just fine, if you don't mind me saying so."

Prudence hesitated.

"They'll be modest. I swear it," Mrs. Perkins assured her. "My Lizzie isn't one to flaunt what the good Lord gave her. I even thought she might join the abbey when she was younger, before she married John, but I'm right glad she didn't or I wouldn't have those grand-babies on the way, now would I?"

Prudence could not help but feel a smile creep across her face. Mrs. Perkins was a breath of fresh air after the silence of the convent. She found that the older woman's chatter eased her tension and allowed her to feel at once at home here at Halthaven.

A short while later, Prudence had washed her hands and face and shook out what dust she could from the grey woolen gown. Her other had been folded away for Mrs. Perkins to deliver to her daughter later that evening. Prudence allowed the housekeeper to comb her hair and twist it up into an intricate knot that she claimed to have learned from a French woman who had passed through the village several years before.

She cast a glance in the looking-glass and determined that she looked as respectable as she was able. With a sigh and a shrug, Prudence allowed herself to be led back down the staircase to meet the baron's young charge.

Marietta was a pretty girl with blonde curls that hung down her back and a vibrant blue gown that matched her eyes. She had a youthful giggle and an easy smile, as if she were pleased to be raised by her relative, despite the tragic loss of her parents. Prudence recalled the housekeeper's tale that the girl had been orphaned at only five years old and had very few memories of her mother and father. Still, she had said, Lord Halthaven did his best to keep the memory of his dear cousin and his wife alive in the child's heart.

When Prudence entered the drawing room, Lord Halthaven was offering his praise for a drawing that the child had completed in his absence that afternoon.

"Your mother too was a magnificent artist," he told her. Marietta looked up at him with a wistful grin, begging that he tell her more.

"What of father?" she asked. "Did he draw?"

"Not a lick," Lord Halthaven laughed. "She once bet him to make a likeness of a fawn he saw in the great wood. Only, when he drew the spots upon its back it looked more like a squat tortoise than anything and she'd not allow him to hear the end of it."

Prudence could not help but laugh herself at the strange tale as she approached the pair. Her quiet chuckle drew the attention of Marietta, who rounded on her with wide, excited eyes.

"Are you Miss Riverford?" She clapped her hands together and bounced on the tips of her toes, like a bird about to take flight. "I am so pleased to make your acquaintance. Cousin George won't let me venture too far from the manor without a proper companion. He thinks I am far too mischievous."

Marietta glanced back over her shoulder and made a face at the baron, which Prudence found quite hard to process. She had never made jokes of her father in such a manner. Her brothers, perhaps, but they were different, kind and lighthearted even.

"You are mischievous," Lord Halthaven replied, with a pointed look that must have reminded the girl of something she had done, for she had the decency to look contrite.

"I suppose I am in need of a companion," she admitted. "Though, I must say, I am pleased to see that you are much younger than the last."

"Marietta," the baron scolded. "Mrs. Rovier was a fine woman."

"Fine, yes," Marietta agreed, "but she'd not allow me to ride, for she said it made her bones ache and her mind addled." The young spitfire turned to Prudence who was now finding great amusement in the conversation. "Do you ride, Miss Riverford?"

"On occasion," Prudence revealed. "Though I am no horsewoman."

"That is well enough for me!" Marietta grinned. "We shall get on just fine, I think."

"You know the rules," he reminded his charge. "You are to stay to the grounds. No exceptions. Understood?"

Marietta groaned. "Just as far as the village, please Cousin George."

"Miss Riverford has no knowledge of the neighborhood," he replied. Prudence was glad that he made no reference to her situation. "You'll stay at Halthaven until further notice." When Marietta seemed disconsolate he reminded her that it was the beginning of the harvest season and her more common friends would be far too busy with the crops to entertain the whims of a lady.

She nodded her head in dismay, blonde curls bouncing, and agreed that she had been notified of their duties. While it appeared that there were many families of note in the Halthaven neighborhood, the properties were far too distant to allow for daily visits. It was all very different from the bustling countryside of Nettlefold where Prudence had spent the majority of her years.

"At least we have the Harvest Ball to look forward to," Marietta concluded with a sigh. "We'll have to find you a better gown than... that," she grimaced at Prudence's simple grey frock.

Prudence felt her eyes grow wide with shock. She had no intention of attending a ball. That would be contrary to everything that the Mother Abbess had instructed. Prudence was to keep as quiet an existence as possible until her removal could be arranged.

Lord Halthaven released a low curse under his breath. The word brought a giggle from his charge and a quick apology from the baron.

"I had not thought on that," he explained. "The Harvest Ball will be held in a month's time, at the conclusion of the picking. There will be nearly a dozen families staying at Halthaven that evening."

"It is no matter," Prudence offered with a shrug. "I expect that the Reverend Mother will have made arrangements for my removal in that time. If not, then I shall have no qualms remaining in my room. I am guessing, Miss Marietta is not yet out?" The girl shook her head. "That settles it. She cannot yet attend such an evening event, and I have no need for a ball."

Marietta scrunched her nose as if to say that she thought it strange that Prudence had no interest in the occasion.

"You can watch from the rail of the stair at my side," she giggled with childish excitement. "I do love to look at all of the beautiful ladies in their gowns and the gentlemen in their fine silk coats."

Prudence could not help but recall the spectacle that her gowns had once made. She decided not to mention them to the child, unless for nothing more than a good laugh. When it seemed that the conversation had run its course, and the gentleman looked antsy to return to his matters of business, Prudence suggested that Miss Marietta show her to the stables where they might check on dear Posey and her wellbeing.

Marietta was thrilled to hear of the arrival of a puppy, having always wanted one for herself. Prudence promised that she might help in the care of the creature, so long as they did their best to teach the animal to be gentle and obedient.

With that, Prudence's hand was grasped and she was pulled from the room before she could offer a word of farewell or thanks to the gentleman. It took no more than a moment for Prudence to recognize that the young Miss would keep her every moment occupied with her vibrancy and excitement.

Perhaps it was for the best, she thought. A little distraction was in order. She might even come to push the horrors of the past to the back of her mind where they could remain thoroughly buried.

The women found Posey curled in a bed of straw behind the locked door of the birthing stall. Prudence thought that it was the perfect pen in which to contain the rambunctious pup until she could be better trained. The last thing that she wished was for the small dog to destroy any more of Lord Halthaven's belongings.

The pair of ladies sat upon the floor of the stall for several hours, talking and plying the animal with treats as incentive to waddle from one lap to another. Prudence was surprised to find that there was much to admire about the young girl who had lost her family at such a young age. Prudence felt a sort of kinship to the child, though their horrors were quite different. It seemed to her to be a difficult task to be a female in this age. Few enough were granted a simple path to comfort and pleasure. Even a title and fortune was no guarantee that one might be protected from strife.

Prudence listened as Marietta burst at the seams with excited rambles in her attempt to tell her new companion everything that there was to know about her life at Halthaven Manor. Prudence could not help but think that it was so very different from the cold and imposing homes in which she had lived.

Though her own mother had tried her best, it had been impossible to provide any sort of lasting comfort under the firm thumb of her tempestuous husband. Instead, the family had slunk around in the shadows and done their best to avoid his wrath.

It took no time at all for the females to find that they

got on just fine. Posey was a bridge that allowed the strangers to focus their attentions upon a mutual task with combined goals. By the time Marietta was called to wash for dinner, the puppy was able to sit upon command and respond somewhat to her own name. All in all, it felt like a victory for Prudence who had for so long craved such simple pleasures.

Lord Halthaven was kind enough throughout the meal, though not overly talkative. Prudence found herself taking a liking to his quiet ways as well. He participated in the conversation, offered a teasing note here or there to incite the laughter of the women, but did nothing to oppress his table-mates. Marietta's voice dominated the supper, and both adults were happy to encourage it.

Prudence allowed the edge of worry in her mind to creep away as she relaxed into the role of companion. That night when she closed her eyes, she could almost imagine that there was nothing else outside of this quiet home. If only it could remain so forever, she thought.

6

*J*asper Numbton, the Earl of Fondleton returned from his visit to London to find his small country Manor in disarray.

"I am sorry, my lord," his steward informed him as soon as his feet hit the cobbled stone of the lane. "We have searched high and low, but she cannot be found. I sent a man to Nettlefold but there has been no sign of her in the village or near her family home."

It took Jasper a moment to process the information that his wife was missing. Though he had been loath to wed one such as she, neither as thin nor as beautiful as he preferred, he possessed enough male pride to be furious that she had the gall to defy him. He had given her wealth and a title, everything a lady could need.

All that he had expected in return was that she remain a dutiful wife and fulfill his every wish and whim. Of course, she could not even do that willingly. That was no matter, he had thought. He liked a little fight in a lady, a little fear in her eyes.

Still, he had thought her obedient enough to remain in wait until his return.

His trip to London had been much needed. He had been craving something new. An acquaintance had told him of a place well-hidden in a quiet neighborhood of London where the girls were young and came at a decent price.

Lord Fondleton, however, was not one who would be seen in such a place. Furthermore, he preferred the challenge of the hunt, to catch his prey with skill and temptation, rather than pay a sum. He fancied himself quite apt at his business. Never a suspicion or claim had been laid to his name. Now that he was wed, he had even more cause to be trusted. Perhaps his forced marriage to the Prudence was not so terrible in that way.

London was a good place to go unnoticed, if one wished it. It was easy enough to come upon a female of questionable ilk if you hung around the places where they were sold. There were always one or two that had been bought, used, and abandoned for the next best offering. Of course, then Jasper could take what he wanted and no one would be the wiser. What gentleman worth his salt would take the word of base slime over an earl?

He had thought to return for a fortnight to handle his matters of estate, and then find a nice quaint countryside to frequent for the holidays with new faces and females to chase. His wife could remain at the Manor, perhaps even with an heir in her womb to make her useful.

Never had he expected that his plans would have to be altered to pursue the minx to whatever end of the countryside she had fled. She must be found so that she might be silenced and his name ensured. Though he allowed the rage to fuel his action, he could not deny that there was an inkling of interest that she had proven to be more resilient than expected.

Such a daring act was beyond most ladies. In fact, it almost made him want her again. He would return her to his care and if he chose to be so kind, she could never be allowed the same freedoms. Still, there was something appealing about having a wife under lock and key. A whisper of a rumor that she was ill would be enough to keep the questions at bay. Then, he could have his way, both within his domain and without.

Lord Fondleton could not suppress the surge of laughter that overtook him.

"My lord?" his steward looked at him with concern. "Are you not concerned?"

"Concerned?" Jasper scoffed. Then his face broke out into an evil grin.

"I am *furious*. Have my items cleaned and packed at once. I leave at first light."

He would find Prudence if it took him a lifetime of searching. She would not best him and make him a fool. No, he thought. She would suffer for her defiance, of that he would be certain. The lady had few enough resources to her name. It would not take him long to discover where she had fled.

He would begin in that drat little town of Nettlefold, where he had first happened upon her. Soon enough he should know all of her family connections. Then, he would smoke her out like a fox from its den.

7

*P*rudence saw little of Lord Halthaven for the first week of her stay, except at mealtimes. He was busy making arrangements for the harvest of his fields, which would supply the manor and its residents with foodstuffs for the upcoming winter season.

She entertained Marietta as best she could considering the girl's energetic disposition. It was fortunate that Posey had been brought along, for many hours were whiled away in the stables with the attempt of training the animal. Marietta had taken her guardian's word to heart when he had promised that Posey might be allowed to sleep at the foot of Marietta's bed once the dog could be trusted inside the Manor. Prudence could not help but applaud what she understood as Lord Halthaven's attempt to give the girl a project upon which to focus her time and energies during a period that would otherwise be filled with boredom.

Marietta missed her friends more than anything. Yet, many of them were well beneath her station and had been set to working for the season. Though she longed to travel to the village to see them, Prudence was happy for the excuse that the town was all but empty these days.

It was a week to the day of her arrival that Mrs. Perkins appeared with a stack of Lizzie's dresses to make Prudence a new gown despite her protests. Her own dress had not been salvageable. She could not bring herself to care. Besides, she was happy to hear that the ruined gown's remaining cloth was promised to be used to outfit a child in the village.

The dress fabrics were plain and the style both muted and modest but Lizzie's hand with a needle made every cut and stitch follow the ample curves of Prudence's form so that her buxom hourglass figure was displayed like a masterpiece. The neckline had been raised demurely, as was to be expected for the preference of a lady of the cloth. Yet, never before had Prudence felt more confidence in an article of clothing.

She cursed away all of those flashy gowns that she had been forced to wear, for fear that she was too plain. Now, with the simplicity of the gown, even one as dull as she might seem to shine above it.

She wondered how it was that that could be possible as she stared at her reflection in the glass. Praise for Lizzie's hand was given to be passed with all her thanks to the woman herself. Of course, she had worked a miracle.

Before she could prevent the thought, Prudence felt the green pallor of jealousy shadow her satisfaction. If such progress could be made on her own features by the skill of a handy seamstress, what sort of fanciful creations might be made for those as beautiful as Prudence's sisters, particularly Temperance or the twins? Prudence felt her heart sink as she wondered if still, even at her best, she did not do the gown its full due service.

She thanked Mrs. Perkins heartily and promised to visit Lizzie at her bedside at regular intervals to provide what little relief she could to the poor mother-to-be in her bouts of boredom.

She was in the process of laying smooth the elegant blue folds that Lizzie had arranged to disguise the fact that the gown had once concealed a protruding womb. The fabric had been tucked and stitched so that it could be re-let if ever the need arose for, of course, the gowns would be returned to Lizzie under the assumption that Prudence would have no need for them upon her return to the abbey.

Prudence pressed her hands to her own stomach and wondered if she had been right to tell the Reverend Mother with such certainty that she was not with child. Though there had been no sign or symptom, she could not be truly sure after so few weeks. The idea that she might be carrying Jasper's child made her ill. Would she feel the draw to return to him for the sake of an heir? Or could she manage to care for another being on her own, without the support of a man? The thoughts raced through her mind until she felt dizzy with panic.

In an attempt to outrun her fear, she turned upon her heel and hastened toward the stables. Marietta was at her studies and what Prudence required more than anything at this moment was a sample of unconditional love.

She knew exactly where to find it.

She felt a wave of relief upon the discovery that the barn seemed deserted and quiet. She did not wish for anyone to witness her in her moment of weakness. She crept along on silent feet and checked the stalls as she passed by. The tears in her eyes were barely restrained. She told herself she need only get to the stall which Posey had come to call home to find relief in her furred companion.

A large bay horse snorted at her side and caused her to start, but Prudence only took a deep breath and scratched the beast along the length of its neck before she moved on.

Just as her hand settled upon the latch to the stall door, she heard a pair of male voices approaching with laughter from the wide opening at the far end of the barn. Still not wishing to be seen, she spun through the door and closed it behind her just before the voices rounded the corner and entered the main aisle of the stables.

Prudence closed her eyes and breathed a sigh of relief as she leaned against the stall door. Her eyes ached from all of the emotions that she had suppressed in recent months. For her entire life, if she were to be honest. She wanted to scream and cry all at the same time, though she would settle for holding Posey close and stroking her velvet soft ears.

"Ah, now you've caught me," came a low voice from the corner.

Prudence's eyes flew open with a wild panic. For an instant, she wondered if her fears pertaining to her dangerous husband had caused him to appear out of thin air, like the magicians on the streets of London might produce a dove or a flower for a lady. How might he have found her and hidden himself away in the very stall in which she found herself at the moment?

"It was never my intention to startle you," Lord Halthaven explained. It took a moment for Prudence to recognize the gentleman seated on a stool in the corner of the stall with a sleeping puppy cradled in his arms.

It all made sense now. Lord Halthaven's voice was much kinder than that of Jasper Numbton's raspy growl. She should have recognized it at once, rather than allowing fear to overtake her at the sound of any male word.

"My lord," she pressed a hand to her breast and began to take slow breaths to calm the racing of her heart. "What are you doing here?"

The baron allowed himself a grimace of embarrassment.

"I am afraid I have been caught in my secret," he laughed. "I have been slipping away almost daily to find a moment of quiet for my thoughts. I was worried that, as a runt, the pup would have difficulty surviving." He explained how he had come to check on the welfare of the animal.

It just so happened that Posey had a fondness for the liver that the chef had been pressing upon the baron with the claim that it would benefit his health. He had been stealing the dish away under the guise of consumption to fatten the happy pup. As the habit developed into a daily excursion, he had found comfort in the solitude. Still, he had not intended to make it known that he had a soft spot for the creature.

Prudence could not help but find the admission endearing. She had come to the stable for the very same reason. Now however, she felt the pressure in her eyes and throat had lessened. She no longer felt the urge to release her tears of agony. She looked upon the comical scene of a respectable gentleman too nervous to make it known that he was attached to a small bundle of fur.

Her own woes were forgotten for the moment as she informed Lord Halthaven that he was welcome to visit Posey as often as he wished.

He made a move as if to transfer the pup to Prudence's care and leave her to her peace. Prudence assured him that he was welcome to stay, and scratched the dog behind its ears while it continued to sleep in the gentleman's arms.

"I am not opposed to the company," she said, and found that she meant it. Were she alone she would likely find herself crying until there were no tears left, locked in her misery. Instead, she felt the lightness of companionship settle upon her. She was happy for it.

They spoke for a long while about Marietta and then the progress in Posey's training that had been improving with each passing day.

Then, Lord Halthaven tilted his head and stared at Prudence with a confused expression.

"You look different," he mused as if he could not put his finger upon the change.

Prudence felt the blood rush to her cheeks. "Lizzie altered some dresses for my use," she explained.

"Ah, yes," he nodded. "That must be it. I have grown so accustomed to your grey curtains that I do believe that this is the first time I have seen you look..." He paused. Prudence wondered if he were about to say that this was the first time he had seen her look like a lady.

"Curtains?" she laughed. Of course that was an accurate description of the quality of the gown that she had been wearing since her arrival. Lord Halthaven had the decency to appear ashamed at his statement, but Prudence could not help but continue to laugh, for she needed it dearly. "I suppose that you are right," she agreed once she had composed herself.

Lord Halthaven paid the obligatory compliment to her new attire but Prudence did not register his words. His features had turned pensive. It was as if he were looking upon her for the first time and seeing something different than before.

It was the goal of a postulant to mute themselves to the point of invisibility. Though, Prudence had always thought herself invisible. Besides, she thought, it was not her wish to catch the eye of anyone, especially not an eligible gentleman who had devoted himself as her protector.

Again, her cheeks flushed and she was forced to look away. She had never once thought of Lord Halthaven as an eligible gentleman until this very moment although, it was clear that he was quite free of any attachments as far as she could tell. She cursed the thought from her mind. She would not, could not, view him in such a manner.

If she did, then she might be forced to admit that he was attractive.

It took all of Prudence's skill to suppress the groan that threatened to creep forth. Her mind was determined to betray her for, now that she had thought it, she could not help but admit that she appreciated the subtle nature of his elegant features. She could not think such things. The baron may be free of attachment, but she was not. Though her husband was loathsome, she was still a legally married woman.

"Are you quite alright, Miss Riverford?" he asked with concern, when she was unable to conceal that she was flustered.

"What? Oh, yes..." she stammered. "It is only that I have a lot on my mind." She had learned enough about his character to feel confident that Lord Halthaven would not press her for further detail. He was used to those that were sent to his care and their preference for privacy. Ever since she had first expressed the desire to keep her tale to herself, he had never brought forth the topic again.

"That is to be understood," he said with a soft tone, as if he truly did understand her state even without the details of her trauma.

She nodded and kept her eyes upon Posey, whose paw was cradled in her hand so that she might rub her thumb in a circular motion through the velvety fur.

"Perhaps we can lighten your mood!" Lord Halthaven suggested with a burst of energy that brought a surprised grin to Prudence's features.

"Oh?" she asked.

"Marietta has been craving a ride but it has been far

too wet with all the rain," he explained. "Today is just the day, I think."

Prudence scrunched her nose as she considered the offer. She was not the finest of horsewomen. Mediocre would be generous.

"You can ride the old mare," he laughed upon witnessing her expression. "She'll not go faster than a trot no matter how you tempt her and she is as calm as a fine summer's day."

"Marietta craves a chase," she replied. It was all the girl had talked about in recent days, the urge to feel the wind in her hair as her own mount sprinted across the fields.

"She might go ahead of us, so long as she remains within sight," he shrugged. "She needs to release her spirit every so often, else I shall have a mutiny on my hands."

"Us?" Prudence asked before she could swallow the question.

"Unless you'd rather not." Lord Halthaven seemed not the least bit offended that the lady might not be comfortable in his presence. In fact, it was that which made her decision.

"I do not mind," she murmured.

"Excellent." He offered a smile. Prudence observed that Lord Halthaven was prone to smiling. It was an unusual habit for a gentleman of note, but she found that she liked it just the same. "I should enjoy the company as I make my observations of the fields."

"You would ride either way!" she cried with a hint of laughter. He had maneuvered her into the offer as well as the finest of peddlers might sell a rock as a gemstone.

He nodded and joined his laughter to her own.

"Now it should be much more pleasant," he offered, "and Marietta will stop pacing between the windows of the drawing room in search of the sun."

It was true that the girl had been doing exactly that. Prudence was surprised to find that Lord Halthaven was far more aware of the young lady's doings than she had thought. For some reason, the knowledge gave her comfort, as if he would do all in his power to ensure her care. On the other hand, had Jasper mentioned an observation of her daily activity, Prudence would have felt at once a bout of paranoia and fear of his intent.

It was strange to her that she might feel such opposite reactions from encounters with two very different gentlemen. She agreed to the ride and left at once to don her borrowed habit and collect the child while Lord Halthaven readied the horses.

It was a fine day for a ride, after all.

Upon hearing the news Marietta, was near bursting with excitement. She flew through the manor with a shout that called her maid to her side as if a fire had been announced. Prudence could not help but laugh at her youthful abandon. She, herself, could never recall such a freedom of spirit. It would never have been permitted of the Baggington children.

Soon, the pair hastened toward the barn, where three fine horses stood saddled and ready. Prudence felt a moment of hesitation. She was petite in height, far too low to the ground to mount with ease. In addition to that her buxom form made her leery of allowing a gentleman or stable boy to hand her up. She knew that it was a silly thing to be concerned with, but still the feeling of panic could not be swayed.

"Come now." Marietta pulled her along. The girl grasped the reins of a sleek filly of midnight hue. The beast stomped her feet, ready to be set loose. She looked as fierce as her young mistress; Prudence knew that she would never be persuaded to mount such an animal.

Marietta slapped a second set of reins against Prudence's palm and gestured that she should follow. The elder looked back and allowed herself a sigh of relief. The docile mare at the other end of the leather strap looked bored and stood as still as a fence post until she was tugged along. Despite the mare's soothing exterior, the arch of her back stood well above Prudence's head. Again, she loathed the thought of clambering atop the mountainous beast. It could not be done without being made a fool, she thought.

Still, she followed Marietta to the far side of the barn where, much to her relief, she saw a set of mounting stairs. Marietta marched right up and leapt sidelong onto her filly. The animal pawed the ground and Marietta whispered in soothing tones a promise that they might soon race against the wind.

Upon cautious feet, Prudence climbed the steps. The mare, well trained to the task, stood close to the platform so that she might sit with ease in the lady's saddle. The task was completed without any harm to her person or her pride. That, in itself, was a victory.

Prudence stroked the mare's mane and scratched

behind her ear to offer her thanks. The mare leaned her head back to increase the pressure of her rider's fingers. Her lazy acceptance told Prudence at once that they would get on without issue.

The sound of hoof beats came from behind, and the ladies were soon joined by the baron, who must have mounted from the ground and without difficulty. Prudence narrowed her eyes and could not help but notice his agile frame. Young enough to be full of vigor, but old enough that he should have already been married. She wondered for a moment about the gentleman at her side.

Perhaps he had been too occupied with his own affairs, or care of his charge, she thought. Still, she determined that there must be something wrong with him to be in his position and as yet unattached. Even she, with all her faults, had managed to be wed. Though, not well, she admitted.

"George," Marietta giggled as she rode circles around the pair, "might I ride ahead?"

"Can you not wait until we have cleared the lane?" he asked. "I should not like you beyond my sight."

"I'll stay to the north pasture until you catch up," Marietta begged. "Oh, please. Look at how she prances. We must run. I promise to be watchful."

They had arrived at the entrance to a tree-arched lane. The sun glistened between the branches for as far as the eye could see. Prudence could tell that Lord Halthaven was hesitant to allow his charge to rush ahead where she might be out of sight for a distance. His sidelong glance in her direction revealed that he too might be considering the immorality of riding alone with a young lady through the canopy.

"Miss Riverford shall not mind," Marietta whined with a pleading look to Prudence. Her tone and statement indicated that she saw no cause for concern as to Prudence's reputation. She was, as far as they knew, soon to be a nun. "Please tell him," she begged.

Prudence opened her mouth but no sound came out. A part of her wanted to give in to the yearning need of the child, to allow her to race with the wind and free her spirit in a way that Prudence herself would never understand. Another part of her recalled that it would be indecent to ride alone with a gentleman that was not her husband. However, the property was very isolated and the chance of observation was as rare as a white stag in the wood.

Her mind recalled the evil grimace of her husband's face and she felt at once the urge to defy him. Prudence could not say where her burst of spiteful rebellion had come from. She found that she not only did not care about protecting her husband's pride, but felt a secret exhilaration in disregarding him.

"Ride on," she allowed. "I have no fear of Lord Halthaven's company."

"You see, cousin?" Marietta squealed with delight.

Lord Halthaven laughed in his deep baritone and gave his nod of permission. No sooner had his chin dipped to his chest that Marietta had kicked her mount into flight and disappeared around the bend.

"I apologize," Prudence offered on second thought. "It

was not my decision to make. I should have deferred to your permission."

"It is of no matter," Lord Halthaven smiled. "So long as you approve, I shall as well. Marietta would not be restrained for long either way. We'd have not heard the end of it until she was set free."

Prudence nudged the mare along so that she might drift ahead in her own thoughts for a moment. She could not say why but she felt a sudden bout of melancholy as she watched the gentleman interact with his charge. He was kind, gentle, and understanding of Marietta's needs. She wondered if the girl knew what a blessing it was to be raised in such a peaceful environment.

"Have I upset you in some way?" Lord Halthaven asked once she slowed and allowed him to draw his horse alongside her once more.

"Not at all," she replied in earnest. "It is only that you, and everyone that I have met at Halthaven, are very kind to the young Miss, and myself, and I wonder how two worlds can exist alongside one another and yet be so different?"

"Is Halthaven so dissimilar to what you have known?" he asked in a quiet tone. It was as if it hurt him to hear as much.

"As different as night and day, my lord. You truly have no idea," she replied with a shake of her head. She regretted the admission at once and could not say what had prompted her to be so honest. Prudence drew her strength around her and reminded herself that it was best to keep her walls hardened. Lord Halthaven seemed good enough to be trusted, but she had learned well that appearances were not always bound in truth.

"I wish that there was more that I could do to help," he murmured.

Prudence looked over to see him watching her with wide, caring eyes. The darkened hue made his gaze seem like a deep abyss that was calling her to dive within and allow him to help bear the burden of her hurt. She could not allow it.

"Lord Halthaven," she began with a sigh.

"Please, call me George." When she did not continue he shrugged. "You are staying at my estate. Formalities seem unnecessary under the circumstances, do you not think?"

Prudence blew out a slow breath.

"Please, I do not wish you to feel obligation," he explained. "It is only that, for some reason, I feel as if there is so much more to know about you. I can't explain it. I've never been bothered to know the others that have stayed in my care, but you do not seem like the rest of them. I cannot put my finger on it. It is almost as if..." he shook his head as if unable to complete the thought. She hoped that he never did. "I don't know. I am sorry. It's silly of me."

"No," Prudence waved away his discomfort. "I'm afraid that I have never much been like others. I suppose that is my greatest flaw."

She looked off into the wood so that she might not see his reaction. Prudence was used to gentlemen viewing her as unworthy compared to the beauties that surrounded them. Not that she cared if Lord Halthaven thought her beautiful, she amended. It was only that she could not believe the words that were flowing so freely from her mouth.

If things kept on in their path of getting to know one another she would be sorely tempted to share at least a small bit of her tale. She should be embarrassed to have been so open with a gentleman that she hardly knew. Still, it felt right. It felt safe, in this moment.

The wood was growing darker as they traveled further along the trail. The foliage from the summer was beginning to change color and soon the leaves would fall to reveal the bright sunshine through the branches above. For now, though, it seemed like an isolated paradise. Two travelers alone in the world, free to speak their hearts without fear.

"You know," Lord Halthaven pursed his lips and spoke in a casual tone, "I think that is what I find most intriguing."

Prudence knew not how to respond. How could this gentleman find her intriguing? No one had ever said as much. It must be a falsehood, she decided. Perhaps he was used to paying compliments out of duty rather than truth. Still, she had not sensed a ploy or lack of verity in his words.

They rode along through the covered lane until the woods opened up to an expanse of fields that were divided into neat rows by a meticulous fence line. Prudence pressed her lips together to prevent herself from commenting on how the maintenance of the land was indicative of the man.

Ahead, they could see Marietta racing along with her

head thrown back and her windswept plait trailing behind her. Prudence admired the girl's spirit and the comfort that allowed such freedoms. She wished, more than anything, to never see it taken away from the sweet and kind Marietta. Not all souls must be crushed or burdened, she hoped.

They rode along the fence posts. Lord Halthaven made notes of the rails that he wished mended or replaced. The tenants were out about their business and stopped to greet the landowner with wide grins and waving hands. Many expressed their pleasure with the season's crops and promised a bountiful harvest for the benefit of all.

To Prudence, everything about this life and this estate seemed like something out of one of the novellas of which her mother had been fond. It was as if this place could have only been created within the depths of one's imagination. Surely, it could not be the norm.

She watched in silence, which raised no concern as a quiet nature was to be expected from one who was supposedly fated to be cloistered.

Marietta joined them after a time, expressing her desire to reunite with her friends once the harvest was complete.

"It has been dismal without them," she explained. "What a blessing that Miss Riverford has come to us, else I would surely have fallen into a state of melancholy."

Prudence was introduced, as Miss Riverford, of course. The tenants welcomed her to the estate and expressed their desire to see her about town during her stay. Lord Halthaven looked uncomfortable at the notion.

Of course, he had promised to keep Prudence free from notice and as far away from the town as possible. It would have been suspect for him to mention that they wished to keep her presence and identity a secret, so he said nothing. Still, a sidelong look to the baron told her all that she needed to know. He would ensure that no rumor began to circulate of the new guest at Halthaven Manor.

8

The weeks went by in much the same way.
Marietta's spirits improved even further as the
rains lessened and she was free to beg a ride nearly once
a day. Lord Halthaven took to joining the ladies in the
afternoon and soon Prudence found that they had grown
close in their friendship. If nothing else she valued his
opinion.

With each passing day their interactions fell into a
natural rhythm and Prudence felt at ease as she had
never before. Under his guidance Posey was becoming a
well-mannered pup, much to Marietta's delight. It would
not be long before the baron would fulfill his promise
that Marietta could bring the creature into the main
house so that the dog might sleep at the end of her bed.

For now, the sound of racing feet and pattering paws
could be heard only in the daylight hours as the pair
chased one another from room to room and down the
long halls. Prudence would find herself chuckling to no

one in particular as she thought that this is what a home was supposed to be.

Temperance had made her appearances but it was not until one fine afternoon that she stayed for more than just a brief observation of her sister's care. The siblings had taken a walk through the gardens and down toward a small pond where they might have some privacy.

"You look well," Temperance observed with a weak smile.

"Thank you," Prudence replied. "I feel almost healed in this place. It is too good to be true. Sometimes, I even forget why I came here or, more aptly, those that had driven me hence."

"I have never forgotten," the novice whispered as if the admission were a secret that she could not bear to voice.

"Not even after all these years?" Prudence had been led to think that this new life of her sister's had been chosen for the safety and healing that it allowed.

"I do not think that it will ever be so, for me," Temperance sighed. "I am happy to hear of your progress. It is all that I could have ever wished for you." Suddenly, Temperance's features softened out of the rigid blankness that she had come to perfect and Prudence caught a sight of the mischievous sister to whom she had once been so close. "It would not, perhaps, have anything to do with a certain gentleman, would it? Lord Halthaven is a good man."

Prudence allowed her jaw to drop open as she chastised her sister for such an assumption.

"Of course not!" she gasped. "I would never dare to

think such a thing of Lord Halthaven. It would be an insult to his kindness and, besides," she added in a hush, "have you forgotten that I am still married."

"A fact of which he is unaware," Temperance grinned. "I have seen the way that he looks at you."

"That is the most absurd thing that you have ever said, Temperance Baggington," Prudence said with an exaggerated tone. "If he looks at me in any way, it is with concern for my wellbeing. There is nothing of interest in such behavior from one who has been given the task of my protection."

"There has been nothing to protect you from," Temperance laughed. "Such concern as you say is without reason so far as I have seen." She nodded with certainty. "He looks upon you as a man might look upon a woman that he admires."

"You are daft." Prudence could not help but laugh at her sister's silly assumptions. "No man has ever looked upon *me* with admiration."

"You have always been far too hard on yourself," Temperance replied. "There is everything about you to admire when you allow yourself to be true. It is only all of this hiding behind pretenses that prevents it."

"I am nothing but pretense here," Prudence laughed. "A runaway lady, unwed, and desirous of a life in the convent. There is nothing of truth in it."

"Yes, but you seem… different than I recall."

"My entire life is different," Prudence explained. "For the first time I am free… of Father… of Jasper… and anyone who might wish to do me wrong."

"Well," Temperance clasped her sister's hands in her

own, "then it was a blessing that you came to us. For that I shall be happy and say my prayers of thanks."

"Temperance..." Prudence hesitated, unsure of how to ask the question after the Reverend Mother had been so stern in her warnings, "are you happy at the abbey?"

"As happy as I think it is possible to be," Temperance replied with an unconvincing shrug. "Where else should I go? Home?" She allowed herself a harsh laugh. "I should think not."

"Why ever not?" Prudence asked. The thought that she might never see her mother or other siblings again was the only thing that had her looking back from time to time. Now that she was well, Prudence worried for their well-being.

"You know exactly..." Temperance began before she was interrupted by a quick tug on the skirt of her woolen gown by a young boy who could not be more than six or seven years old.

"Excuse me Misses," he touched the brim of his small hat with respect. "I been sent to tell you tha' the wagon is ready and all loaded up with supplies for the abbey. We'd best get going if we're to get the cart back by nightfall."

"Of course," the ladies nodded and turned toward the manor at once. Prudence was disappointed that they could not continue their conversation further. She decided to wait for another opportunity to convince Temperance that her life need not be resigned to isolation if she wished it to be otherwise.

Even though Prudence had been unable to attain such peace along her own path, there was still a part of her that hoped for such a future for her siblings. She hugged her sister farewell, a sign of affection that was only just beginning to feel natural once more. With a wave of her hand she bid farewell. As the cart drove away, Prudence felt that her mind was overflowing with the effects of their conversation. She had much to consider.

Could it be possible that Lord Halthaven looked upon her with admiration? She would need to pay better attention in the future, she determined, for such sentiment was not to be encouraged. She was a married woman, after all.

---

9

*L*ord Fondleton felt the demon of rage rise within him. The darkened room of the inn was beneath him in fashion, but he had done his best to keep a low profile so that his wife might not grow suspicious of his repeated attempts to locate her. He hated the filthy room with its rotten floorboards and flea-ridden mattress.

Perry slept in the bed without hesitation once Jasper had resigned himself to the creaking armchair. He had already decided that this night would be the last. He could not be convinced to spend another evening in such squalor. An earl deserved better. Tomorrow they would move on to the next town to make their inquiries under the ruse that they were devoted brothers in search of their addled sister who often wandered away without any hope of recalling the way home.

"What do you mean she cannot be found?" he growled. The clay pitcher that had held water for washing only an hour or so before shattered beside the cowering fool's head. Perry whimpered. He was well aware of his lord's temper, which had been increasing day by day.

"I... I'm sorry, m'lord," he mouthed with little more than a whisper. "Perhaps the next town will..."

"Stop your blithering, you fool!" Lord Fondleton spat. "We've not heard a whisper of her movements no matter the town. A wench does not disappear for weeks on end without the aid of someone with connections. We need to discover her source."

"Y-yes, m'lord."

Jasper could not bear to look upon his sniveling servant for one more moment. They had made no headway in their search by Perry's inspections. On the morrow, he would begin the interrogations himself. He felt a pit of disgust grow in his stomach. His wife had neither the skill nor the connections to evade his wrath. It was only a matter of time before he caught wind of her trail.

"Shall I call for your supper?" Perry asked. Jasper laughed in his servant's face. His favor was not so easily renewed.

"I'll find my own at the tavern." He flung his cloak about his shoulders and headed for the door without a backward glance. He needed a breath of fresh air and a release... of his tensions.

"What of me, m'lord? Shall I join you?"

Lord Fondleton rolled his neck until it cracked. The sound reverberated against the barren walls of the hovel.

"I think not," he replied with a snarl. "Perhaps a

supper foregone will renew your motivation for my purpose."

Perry sputtered some sort of explanation as to why he had had little success in his search. Jasper did not remain around long enough to hear it. He cared not what the servant had to say. He cared less whether or not the man went hungry for his failure. Sympathy for the poor bloke's plight was not at the forefront of his mind at the moment.

His frustration needed to be unleashed. If not upon Prudence, then some other in her stead. She would get her due in good time. Until that prized moment of victory, Jasper would hunt a lesser prey.

The giggling sound of a trio of barmaids calling patrons from the corner matched the tinkling of coin in his pocket. It would take almost no effort at all to draw one away from the others with the lure of his status and purse. A lowly maid was always hopeful that some lord or other would fall madly in love and sweep her away from the dregs of her current existence and into the glitter and ease of high society.

Jasper knew well to play upon that romantic fascination. Then, when the first rays of sunshine revealed the stark truth of his deception, the wench would keep quiet for fear of slander and ruin.

He felt a cold laughter simmer within him but suppressed its release and opted for a charming smile instead. Two fingers tipped the brim of his hat as he nodded to the ladies. With no less provocation they were trotting across the street to beg his patronage in their father's establishment.

Sisters, he thought. All the better. Perhaps he might select more than one for his pleasure. It would take masterful skill to pull off the feat, to be sure. Separate the sheep from the comfort of their flock and then set upon them one-by-one like a wolf to a feast. A true challenge. One he had never attempted before.

He bowed low to make their acquaintance and allowed them to surround him with their smiles and pleasantries as they guided him toward the tavern.

"Beautiful ladies like you ought not to be unattended on the main street," he said.

The three of them tittered like doves, their laughter as music to his ears. He wondered how their screams would sound.

"Oh no one in town will bother us," one said as she took his arm.

"Daddy wouldn't let anything 'appen to us," the second one said while the other sister just batted her very long lashes.

Oh, how to choose, Jasper thought with a thrill of excitement, for the chase was on. He decided that there was nothing to be done about it. He would have them all, and their daddy be damned.

10

A sprinkle of rain, no more than a mist across the dreary fields, awoke Prudence from where she had fallen into slumber upon the picnic blanket. The cushion of tall grasses and wild flowers had provided the perfect sanctuary for their afternoon brunch. Posey had taken to retrieving small reeds and branches from the lush grass to chew at her leisure. Anything within range of her tether was at risk to the destructive teeth of the growing pup.

"Mari," Prudence called with a yawn as she stretched her hands above her still-waking head. "We ought to gather our things before the skies unleash their fury. I did hear the stable master say it was supposed to be a fine day. Never wager upon the English weather, my brother used to say."

Her words were met with silence.

"Marietta?"

Prudence sat up and craned her neck to see beyond

their matted patch of field. The grasses spread before her in every direction with nothing but the distant wood to catch her eye.

"Marietta!" she called once more. Still, her cry received no response. "Miss Marietta, show yourself at once!"

Panic set in and Prudence shoved her feet back into her boots, yanked the laces tight, and grabbed Posey beneath her arm so that she might set off at a full run toward the manor. She would send a servant back for the picnic supplies, if she remembered. She dared not waste a single moment collecting the items when it was clear that Marietta was nowhere to be found.

The shortcut across the fields left her gown wrinkled with a spattering of burrs across the folded skirts. Lizzie would have to mend a tear or two along its length where her underskirts were beginning to show through. Prudence did not care whether or not her attire was in any decent state for viewing. She rushed headlong into the study where she was certain to find the baron reviewing the ledgers at this hour.

True to his regular schedule, the gentleman was alone at his desk on the far end of the room. Prudence had burst through the door with such force that his attention was drawn at once. His eyes opened wide with alarm at the sight of her frightened features. Posey struggled to be released from her captor's trembling clutches.

"Miss Riverford," Lord Halthaven stood with such an abrupt motion that his chair might have spilled over if he had not reached out to stop its plummet toward the polished floor. "What is the matter? You look as though you have seen a ghost."

"Far worse, I am afraid," she murmured. Posey raced across the room, leash in tow, to clamp her jaws upon the curtain length for a raucous tug. "Oh," she cried, "I've made such a mess of things."

"Take a breath," he replied with a soothing tone, but Prudence could not be soothed. She covered her face with her hands and shook her head in despair. The telltale sound of shredding fabric only made the matter worse. The curtain would be ruined for certain. "Tell me what has happened. Are you in danger?"

Prudence shook her head and groaned. It was thoughtful of the baron to worry after her safety. Of course, as far as he was aware she was the only one in any danger.

He waited with a calm, assertive patience for her answer while he disentangled the dog from her destruction. With Posey settled for the moment by a soothing scratch behind the ears, Prudence forced a deep breath and collected her thoughts.

"We went for a picnic and I fell asleep," Prudence admitted with a groan. "Oh George, what have I done?"

"Miss Riverford," Lord Halthaven began, attempting to cut off her ramblings.

"I should never have closed my eyes, but it promised to be such a fine day..." She continued, near tears.

"Prudence," Lord Halthaven said more forcefully, catching her hand. "What in the world are you talking about?"

"Marietta," she cried. "When I woke she was nowhere to be found."

Lord Halthaven's shoulders straightened, and Prudence could sense his urgency.

"When did you last see her?" he asked.

"She was playing with Posey at my side when I drifted off," Prudence explained. "It couldn't have been more than a half an hour, I am sure of it. When I woke, she was nowhere to be found and my calls went unanswered."

"Did you see anyone?" he asked. "Was there any sign of wrongdoing?"

"Not that I noticed," she replied. "It was as if she just disappeared. She wouldn't have wandered off without telling me; I am sure of it."

"No," he agreed. "She knows better than that."

It could only mean one thing. Foul play.

Prudence was beside herself with worry. A young girl about in the countryside on her own did not bode well, particularly with Jasper Numbton on the loose.

"You must wait here, in case there is word," Lord Halthaven instructed. Prudence argued against it but he would not take her with him. Besides, the baron reminded her, he would be faster alone on horseback.

She could not help but feel responsible for whatever harm befell the sweet girl. It was, after all, Prudence who was supposed to be watching after her. She begged that Lord Halthaven bring Marietta home safe and wished his horse speed and his eyesight be keen. She prayed fervently that Marietta was unharmed.

Posey was thrust into her arms as Lord Halthaven raced toward the stable without a backward glance. A small, selfish part of her mind was disappointed to think that he might never look upon her with respect after such a blunder. She pushed the thought as far away as she might, though it lingered against her will. The only thing of importance in this moment was Marietta's safe return.

She stroked the small animal, both for its comfort and her own. If she threw the curtains open she could see a long way down the pebbled path that led to the manor despite the rain that had now begun in earnest. Prudence pulled Lord Halthaven's plush lounger closer to the window so that she might look out without interruption.

There, she perched with eyes peeled for any sign of movement as she awaited his return. Posey curled upon her lap for a snooze, but Prudence felt as if she herself might never sleep again. It was, of course, that evil which had got her in this situation to begin with.

She had grown too comfortable with her host and his young cousin, even trusting herself to relax and slip away in her moments of calm. Never before had she allowed such terrible behavior, such informality. Now, more than ever, she had reason to put a stop to it.

Her own carelessness had been the root of the issue. If only she had maintained the walls that had done so well to protect her for all these years, she might never have let her guard slip. Then, she thought, Marietta might now be safe inside the manor.

IT WAS SEVERAL HOURS LATER AND THE RAIN HAD SUBSIDED when a lone figure came skipping up the path as if nothing were amiss. Prudence stood to look better from the window. She was afraid that her eyes might be deceiving her. Marietta looked happy as could be, without a care in the world, while the entire manor had been turned on its head in the search for her.

Prudence called to Mr. Perkins, the butler, so that he might have word sent to Lord Halthaven, wherever he might be. Then, she rushed from the manor to meet the child at the front stoop.

"Where in God's name have you been?" Prudence asked before Marietta could say a word. "How could you disappear like that without a word? We've all been ill with worry for you."

"Oh no!" Marietta's face fell and her eyes grew wide with concern. "Is George cross? Did you not read my note?"

"What note?" Prudence flung her hands in the air with exasperation. There had been no note, of that she was certain.

"Posey must have eaten it," Marietta shook her head with a groan.

"Oh, we are placing blame upon a puppy now, are we?" Prudence said with disbelief as she thought of the runt sleeping in front of the fire as they spoke. Posey was prone to eating papers, but it did little to excuse Marietta's disappearance for hours at a time.

"Honest," Marietta made a cross over her heart with one finger. "I left a note that my friends were playing in the next field over and I just had to see them. I didn't expect to be gone long, but when the rain started Martha's mother insisted that I wait it out. She did not wish me to catch my death. Besides, I thought you had the letter so I did not think that there was any cause for worry."

"No cause for worry!" Prudence exclaimed. "We've all been worried half to death and Lord Halthaven has been out in that very rain searching for you!"

"Is he terribly cross?" Marietta asked in a small voice.

"I imagine so," Prudence replied.

She had yet to witness George in a fit of anger, but if her own experience was to be any judge of it, she imagined that the man could be nothing less than furious. The thought sent a shiver of fear down her spine. "Come in and we shall prepare you for bed," she said as she placed an arm across the girl's shoulder.

"George will wish to speak with me first," Marietta said with her head hung low.

It was exactly that thought which had prompted Prudence to rush Marietta to her rooms. Perhaps if the gentleman had the opportunity to calm down for an evening, he might be less angry in the morning. It was not likely, she thought, but worth a try.

The least that she could do was remove the girl from his sight for the time being. Then, perhaps Prudence could talk some sense into him, or even bear the brunt of his anger herself. That, she determined, was the least that she could do for the child who she could see now had really meant no harm.

"Off you go," she instructed. Marietta raced up the staircase to follow the command while Prudence peered out the door for any sign of the baron's return. It would not be long. She returned to the study where the dog still slept under the light of the fire.

"Posey, did you eat that note?" she asked as she paced back and forth along the elegant rug.

The dog yawned and rolled over, but seemed content in her comfort. Not a repentant bone in her body. As she waited, Prudence had to remind herself not to bite her nails, a nervous habit that she had developed as a child and never quite mastered. Instead, she clutched at her crumpled skirts in order to keep her hands busy.

It was not long before Lord Halthaven burst into the room. He left a sodden trail in his wake, but seemed to care little for the fact that he was soaked quite through.

"Where is she?" He asked in a low tone that made Prudence bristle.

Prudence squared her shoulders and set her chin, before informing him that Marietta was preparing to retire for the evening.

Lord Halthaven called over his shoulder with a voice that brought Mrs. Perkins at a run. He instructed that his charge be brought down to the study before she was tucked into bed. Prudence felt a wave of despair. The girl would not escape his wrath despite her best attempts. She knew not where to begin.

She opened her mouth to speak, but the firm set of his jaw told her that it was best not to interfere in this moment. Marietta could explain the tale herself, but Prudence refused to let any harm befall the girl despite her misguided tendencies.

The study remained silent until there was a quiet rap on the door that announced the robed child's entrance.

"Oh, George, I've never been so sorry in all my life," Marietta whimpered. "I had no idea you thought me missing."

"I believe I've been *very* clear as to the rules regarding your ventures from the grounds," he replied in a firm tone. "You have deliberately disobeyed me."

Marietta burst into the tale of her misdeed. She took full responsibility for her actions and the knowledge that she should not have wandered off at the first. She also explained the she had thought that the note would suffice if her companion woke before her return. She had intended to return forthwith, although fate and the weather had intervened.

"It is inexcusable," Lord Halthaven concluded. Marietta bowed her head and nodded in agreement. She professed her sorrow and assured her guardian that it would never happen again.

The pair stared at one another for a long while and Prudence knew that all that could be said had been laid forth. Now, she had learned, the punishment would commence.

"Come here, child," Lord Halthaven instructed.

A single tear slipped down Marietta's cheek as she began to take slow steps forward.

Prudence could not help but gravitate toward the pair in anticipation of the coming events. Her heart pounded in her ears, and she felt as if she, too, were a child about to be chastised. It was amazing that no matter how many years she possessed, she always felt like a small girl when confronted by the anger of a grown man.

Lord Halthaven made her even more leery, for he

seemed far too calm and collected in this moment. Her father had been much the same. He would give the appearance of rationality until the moment when his temper would explode into an uncontrollable rage. If ever the Baggington children thought that their father had seen reason, it was not long before they were shown otherwise.

Prudence watched with trepidation as Marietta stepped toward the towering gentleman. With each passing moment Prudence felt even more on edge. She wondered if Marietta knew what to expect, or if she had ever been punished before.

As his hand raised from his side and toward the air between them, Prudence could no longer contain herself. Her instinct took over and without thinking, she thrust herself between the pair, shielding Marietta with her own body.

"I shall take her punishment," she gasped. Her jaw was clenched and her brow furrowed as she prepared herself for the blow.

The moment stretched on as if an eternity, with Lord Halthaven's hand suspended between them. She closed her eyes and turned her face to offer her cheek. Still, the blow did not come.

"Miss Riverford, what is the matter?" Marietta asked behind her.

She heard Lord Halthaven shift and so opened her eyes to ensure that he might not attempt to slip around her. One arm reached for the child at her back and pulled her close.

Her gaze turned back to the gentleman who had

shifted to cross his arms. His jaw was set and his brow furrowed, but not in anger. First, in confusion, which then melded into realization, as he discovered what it was that Prudence had anticipated.

"Come here, Marietta," he said. One arm bent so that he might pinch the ridge of his nose. All of a sudden, he seemed weary.

Prudence was loathe to allow the child to approach, but Marietta showed no sign of the fear, only concern for Prudence herself.

"Yes, George," Marietta murmured. "I am so very sorry."

"I know that," he replied in a soft tone. Again, he raised one hand.

His eyes connected with those of Prudence before he moved any further so that she might follow the slow motion of his limb. Then, to her everlasting surprise, he brushed the wayward hairs from Marietta's face and cupped her cheek so that she might feel his comfort as he spoke. He was gentle, and Marietta pressed her own hand over the top of his, as if they often stood in such a way when having an important conversation.

"I hope you understand how worried we all were that some harm might have befallen you. It isn't safe to be running off like that, even to visit friends," he intoned.

"I know." Marietta nodded. "I never meant to cause alarm. It will never happen again. You have my word."

"Get some rest," he said with a sigh. Marietta leaned up to the tips of her toes and pressed a soft kiss to her cousin's cheek. With one last murmured apology to her companion, she slipped from the study and off to her chambers.

Prudence found that she had been holding her breath for the last of the exchange. It was as if her brain were unable to process what she had just witnessed. Had the gentleman just succeeded in teaching his charge her lesson without aggression or even outright scolding? Marietta had seemed contrite, of that there could have been no doubt.

Lord Halthaven had been stern and serious in his demands, but never given into the anger that Prudence had come to assume simmered beneath the surface of every gentleman's façade. It was as if she had seen a spirit of the forest, or some mythical creature that was beyond explanation. She could not make sense of it.

Her mind was reeling as she turned to follow Marietta from the room. She had no words. Nothing to describe the kind and benevolent instruction that she had just witnessed.

"Prudence," George's voice called after her as her hand settled upon the knob of the door.

She grimaced and did not turn to look his way, though neither did she take another step forward. She waited for him to speak. She could hear that he had approached the fire where Posey slept. Again, she was overcome with worry for the fate of the animal. Would the blame lie there instead? She turned upon her heel to see the gentleman crouched beside the sleeping form, his large hand stroking the fur until it was smooth and the pup released a sigh of contentment.

"Perhaps we ought to have a word," he said in a low voice without looking up.

"George, I…" she knew not where to begin. Nor did she wish to explain her fears and see the disappointment, or disgust, written upon his face. The last thing that she wanted was for this gentleman to see her as damaged or unclean. "I would rather we did not," she admitted in a small voice.

He raised his eyes to meet her own. Her breath caught in her throat as she saw none of the things that she expected there. Instead, his smile was soft and understanding.

"Alright then." He nodded and pressed his lips together, as if he would say no more. Then, unable to allow the moment to pass without clarification, he blurted, "I do not know what sort of terrors you have experienced in your life, Miss Riverford, but I can assure you of one thing beyond a doubt. I would never raise my hand against a lady. Neither you, Marietta, nor any other have reason to fear me. You are safe in my care, and always shall be."

Prudence released the breath that she had been holding, but could not force a response past the lump in her throat. Instead, she nodded her head, dipped into a slight curtsy, and sped from the room. Her eyes welled with unwanted tears that threatened to spill before she reached the safety of her chamber.

She had heard many a gentleman profess such a statement, time and time again. Never before had she believed it. This time, she did. There was no doubt in her mind that Lord Halthaven had been true in his promise, that he was a gentleman of the truest form.

It was in that moment that she felt an ache as the shell of her heart began to crack. Despite all reason and attempts to will it otherwise, the goodness of his character spoke directly to the hurt in her soul, and she had begun to fall in love with the man.

11

———————

The Harvest Ball approached as the weather cooled and the fields were stripped of their bounty. Posey began to settle to the point where she might be trusted to sleep upon the foot of Marietta's bed without risk of destruction.

Prudence found herself spending more and more time with the Baron Halthaven. She was fascinated by this gentleman who was everything opposite of what she had known.

She knew that it was wrong. That she should not allow the emotion that she felt blossoming within her. She would remind herself that she was a married woman, but the memory of Jasper and her previous life seemed so distant that she could almost convince herself that he was no longer a threat to be feared.

If only she could stay in this moment, everything would be perfect.

She could sense that George wished to ask her more about her reactions, and the past that she was running from, but he held his tongue. Still, it was as if they had reached some sort of understanding of one another. It was as if they knew each other's soul. He was cautious and aware to keep his distance and allow her ample personal space, though sometimes Prudence wished that he would give in to the longing that she might glimpse from time to time when he thought that she could not see.

Prudence learned that Lord Halthaven's gentle, but firm, ways were not limited to his dealings with his charge. His tenants held him in the highest of esteem. He was not only respected, but honored for his kindness. Smart enough not to be taken for a fool, and understanding enough that one might ask for his aid in a time of need.

She understood now why the Mother Abbess had placed so much trust upon her nephew's young shoulders. He was a gentleman of rare form; as they all professed to be, but so many fell short.

THE AFTERNOON WAS RIPE WITH THE BEAUTY OF AUTUMN splendor. Prudence found herself breathing in the scent of the crisp leaves and the brittle grasses like a balm to the hurt of her soul.

Her chin was perched upon the cross of her hands as she leaned fully against the top rung of the fence that contained a herd of milk cows. With her eyes closed she allowed her other senses to soak in the world around her. Marietta could be heard off in the distance calling down upon the animals from her vantage point in a tree that overhung the pasture.

A warm breath brushed her face and before she could retreat Prudence felt a surge of wet pressure against her cheek.

She scrunched her nose and laughed, turning her face into her shoulder to protect against the gentle nudges of the cow. The animal sniffed at the twist of her hair that was piled atop her head and then moved on, deeming her curls unfit as a future meal.

"It is good to hear you laugh," George said as he came to lean in a similar fashion upon the next fencepost down. He looked out over the fields. This allowed Prudence to pretend that she had not heard his statement, if she so wished. Though there was no one else in earshot that he might have been speaking to.

"It's easy here," she admitted.

Finally, he turned toward her. "Are you happy?" he asked.

Prudence was caught off guard by the question. She could not ever remember, in her entire being, ever having been asked something so simple as if she were happy. Well or ill, hungry or with thirst, warm or chilled. Of course those things had been asked in abundance, but never once could she recall being asked if she were happy. She took a long time to consider her answer, as well as its implications, before she continued. With a sigh, she decided that she was ready to be honest, in part.

"I am happier now than I think I have ever been in my lifetime," she said with a shrug as if it were no matter.

"I imagine most ladies would be bored with our simple life," he added. "Though, I suppose it is not so different from the abbey. Perhaps, even a bit more lively, I should hope."

"Simplicity suits me," Prudence replied.

"I suppose that is what makes you wish to join the sisters," he mused. "Or, is there more to it than that?"

"I suppose I do not seem very pious," she laughed.

"I find that overt piety is more often an act that not," he muttered. "The best nuns in the abbey are nothing more than regular people with a love for their faith. At least, that is what my aunt always says."

"A fair observation," she agreed. "Your aunt is a very wise woman."

Prudence stood upon the precipice of truth. She wanted more than anything to tell Lord Halthaven that she had no desire to be a nun, could never be. She knew that he longed to know her reason, and passion, for such a lifestyle. She could not bear to lie aloud to one whom had only shown her kindness and truth himself. Yet, her truth would bring forth an entirely different set of questions that she dared not face.

"You have not answered my question," he teased.

"My skill at avoidance is not so neat as some, I see," she laughed. "Alright, I will tell you true." She took a deep breath and collected her courage. Without the idea of her joining the convent between them, Prudence would need to be even more careful not to encourage Lord Halthaven's affections. She was still wed, though she could not bring herself to tell him so much, else she would also need explain her fear of Jasper. Those horrors were still too fresh to speak aloud. "I have no wish to join the abbey, nor have I ever. The novice that visits is my eldest sister. I came to Halthaven because she was the only person that I could think of that might take me in."

"Take you in from what?" His voice was a bare whisper as if he wished not to scare her away from the conversation, yet very much wished to know more.

She shook her head. "I have already said more than I ought. I promised the Mother Abbess to keep my silence and here I am saying too much."

"Then, say no more," he nodded. "Only know your words are safe with me."

"Of that I am fully aware." Prudence could not help but offer him a small smile. He was the closest thing to a true friendship that she had ever experienced. She had the utmost faith that her revelations would go no further.

"On a brighter note," Lord Halthaven stood and clapped his hands together as if to signify that the conversation might move onward, "I have spoken with my aunt about the Harvest Ball and she agrees that there no reason that you ought not attend. The event is within the confines and safety of my properties and is not the sort of thing that draws much attention from those outside of our neighborhood."

"Perhaps that is so," she replied, "but I still see no reason to step forth in a crowd when..." She stopped herself before she could reveal that any number of guests might know the well-traveled and deviously charming

Earl of Fondleton. "No." She shook her head. "I still do not think it a wise idea."

"She asked that I might deliver this letter," he said with a proffered envelope marked with the Halthurst Abbey seal. "She seemed to think it might bring you some relief."

Prudence took the letter with trembling fingers. She knew that Lord Halthaven was thinking along a similar train of thought; that there might be news within that promised that the danger had passed and she was free of all she ran from.

The wax peeled away in one smooth piece, having only been set that morning it was not yet brittle to the touch.

Inside was the elegant script of the Mother Abbess as she set about the task of explaining all that had transpired in the weeks since Prudence had arrived on her doorstep. Many of the names and titles were unknown to Prudence's own recollection. If nothing else she could see that the nun had stitched together an elaborate network of valuable resources during her time at the abbey.

"I see," Prudence murmured with her best attempt at disguising the unexpected wave of disappointment, washing away the happiness that had once pervaded the sunny afternoon.

"What is it?" George asked.

"Well, it explains why she sees no fault in my attendance of the ball," she said with a shrug. She handed the letter over so that he might peruse the contents for himself. "I shall be leaving the day next for an undisclosed location to start my life anew."

She should have been happy. She should have felt nothing but relief and gratitude that the Reverend Mother had been able to find a place that was safe from the reaches of Jasper Numbton and his wicked ways. She should have been happy, but she was not.

The idea that she would soon leave this place brought a lump to her throat. Even Lord Halthaven seemed unable to formulate a response as he did his best to hide the disappointment that flickered briefly across his face.

"You shall go then," he murmured. It was more statement than question. They both knew that she must.

"It appears so," she replied. Prudence tucked the letter into the waist fold of her gown. There seemed much left unsaid between the pair, but there was no point in saying anything else now. Soon enough she would be gone and she might never lay eyes upon George or Marietta again.

"Well," he took a fortifying breath and did his best to reveal a convincing smile. "The Harvest Ball shall double as your farewell. You must attend. I shall not take no for an answer."

She had no way to decline without speaking more upon her departure. If he would lead the way for the appearance of a happy farewell, she would follow suit. Though it seemed a fool's errand to celebrate what was sure to be a heartbreaking evening as she prepared to leave this peaceful life forever; perhaps she might look forward to one last happy memory.

"Alright," she said with a firm nod. "If the Mother

Abbess approves, then I shall make the best of my final hours here in Halthaven." Lord Halthaven offered his arm so that they might walk to collect Marietta from her tree. He spoke of the festivities with renewed excitement, promising that it would be the best Harvest Ball that the town had ever seen. Prudence could almost bring herself to pretend that she looked forward to the event.

---

12

*T*he preparations for the ball were bittersweet. Prudence was forced to fight back tears every time that she thought about leaving the serenity that she had found in this quaint little estate. Lizzie threw herself into the making of the going-away gown, though her swollen fingers were beginning to promise the coming on of her labor in the approaching weeks.

"I've never seen anything so beautiful," Prudence exclaimed with a sigh of pleasure at the sight of the elegant gown.

The delicate ivory overlay glistened in the light as the tiniest beads that Prudence had ever laid eyes upon created an ethereal dusting of reflective shimmer that seemed to float around the gown, rather than adhere to it. "It is as if you've captured a snowfall under the full moon!"

Lizzie laughed.

"Well, I am glad you like it," she clasped the hands of

her friend who had grown most dear in their quiet visits. "It is my first attempt at beading. Mother helped, as well as my cousin, Rose. Together it was not a chore in the least. We talked and laughed and I almost forgot that I am tied to this blasted bed. Though, I cannot tell a lie, there were moments when I nearly pitched the entire thing."

"How could you?" Prudence cried. "It is a masterpiece. I shouldn't wear it, you should save it for yourself."

"Nonsense," Lizzie replied. "Lord Halthaven has paid me well for my efforts. This gown was made for you and I expect you to keep it."

Prudence forced her mouth closed as it had been left to hang open in her shock. She had not known that George had been paying for the use of her wardrobe, or the commission of such a fine gown. She was happy for it, because it made Lizzie's effort well worth her time. The young mother-to-be could use the funds though Prudence had had none herself to offer, and any talk of repayment had been refused with a firm scowl.

"Don't be cross," Lizzie winced. "Lord Halthaven made me promise not to tell. He knew that you would never accept the kindness."

"I am glad for your sake," Prudence replied. "It is only that I do not know how I shall ever repay him for all that he has done."

"You need not," the seamstress said with a shrug. "We have all been glad to have known you. The best you could do is go on toward your own happiness, and do not forget us."

"I shall never forget you," Prudence promised with her whole heart. "Not a single one."

There could be no promise of letters or further visits for the Mother Abbess had made clear that once Prudence vacated Halthaven she was to wash her hands of all she had once known and start anew. Any further contact or tie might only work to lead Lord Fondleton to her place of hiding.

She pressed a kiss to her friend's cheek and thanked her a thousand times over for her skill and thoughtful care in the creation of the prized gown. Even though she had yet to don the item, Prudence knew that it would be the most beautiful thing that she had ever, or would ever, wear in her lifetime.

Marietta was saddened that she could not attend the ball at her companion's side. To relieve her sadness, Prudence helped her make comfortable a vantage point from the top of the stair. They set pillows and blankets against the rail so that Marietta might look down upon the crowd as the ladies arrived in their beautiful gowns and the men in their fine silk coats. Prudence promised to wave up to the girl whenever she passed, so that Marietta might feel a part of the festivities.

"When I am older I want to look just like you," the petite blonde twirled about the room with one of the elder's day gowns pressed to her front as if to wear.

"Don't be silly," Prudence laughed. "You shall be beautiful and Lord Halthaven will ensure that you have the most fashionable gowns to set off your fine features."

"Exactly," Marietta replied with a nod as if they were in agreement. "I shall look just like a picture, like you!"

Prudence could not help but be overcome with confusion. She was not beautiful. No one had ever thought to call her so and, though she did prefer the simplicity of her current style, she would never encourage one as impressionable as Marietta to wish herself a muted experience.

"Don't clench your jaw like that," the child scolded. "You look as if you don't believe a word I say!"

The admonishment in her tone was sincere. Marietta was truly offended that Prudence thought her opinion flawed.

"It is only..." Prudence began. She was cut off before she could form the thought, which was a relief because she knew not what to say.

"Don't be modest," Marietta gaped with an exaggerated roll of her head. "Everyone has seen how George looks at you, and he doesn't look at *anyone* that way. I'd call you a rare beauty. Unconventional, perhaps, but mesmerizing in the unique frame of your features. I would know, I am an artist after all."

Marietta made her speech with such a nonchalance as she picked at a loose thread in the seam of the gown with which she was playing, that Prudence could not help but believe that she meant every word. She knew not how to unpack the knowledge that came in such a short delivery.

Her heart thumped in her chest. It beat a rhythm all its own, like a trumpeter that had abandoned his group and gone off to his own tune. She felt a giddy, nervous sensation that she dared not evaluate. After all, she would be leaving on the morrow. It was best not to think too much on the lessons that she had learned about herself during her stay at Halthaven. Nor about the gentleman who was the source of much of that knowledge.

Prudence fell silent as she completed her preparations for the ball with the boisterous girl at her side. Marietta was lively enough that she took no notice of her companion's pensive attitude.

From the floor below, they could hear the guests begin to arrive as they were greeted at the door by their host. Prudence was determined to wait until the crush had arrived so that she might slip into the crowd unnoticed.

She was not well known in the community and was thankful that she ought not be required to fulfill any of the hosting duties. Lord Halthaven would be busy enough with that task. She might venture to the ballroom for a set or two before slipping back up the staircase to join Marietta behind the bannister.

"You look like an angel," Marietta crooned as she pinched the lady's cheeks and straightened the silver comb that had been leant from the young miss's own collection.

"Hush now," Prudence replied. "There is no need for flattery." Still, she kissed the girl upon the head before preceding her to the stair with a lightness in her heart from the kind word. Marietta took her place upon her cushioned throne and gave an excited wave toward the waiting staircase. With a quivering breath, Prudence stepped forward to look down upon the party below.

Dozens of couples milled about as they waited for the

music to begin. One lone lady descending a stair would go unnoticed soon enough on such a night. Her eyes scanned the crowd and saw not one familiar face. In such a crowd she might enjoy herself without fear that word might return to Nettlefold, or worse, Jasper. They had even contrived a false relation for the evening; Miss Prudence Riverford was to be a distant cousin to Baron Halthaven, thrice removed. With a sigh of relief, she placed her hand upon the bannister and began to make her way to the lower floor.

Halfway between the landing and the main floor, she noticed a figure move to the wide, carved pillar that marked the end of the rail. Her eyes traveled from the shine of his shoes to trim hips and further still to steadfast shoulders, where she eventually came to meet the warm gaze of none other than Lord Halthaven himself.

Despite her determination to repress it, a smile broke forth and she found herself beaming down upon his happy face.

He offered a nod, as a true gentleman might, and awaited her approach with a proffered arm. When her feet descended the final step, she slipped her fingers into the curve of his elbow and allowed herself a shaky breath.

"You look magnificent." He leaned close so that she might hear him over the roar of the crowd.

She could feel the blush heating her cheeks as she made some offhanded comment about his need to attend to his guests. Even to her own ears her words fell flat for it was clear that George had eyes for only one in attendance. Never before had Prudence felt more welcome and adored. It was nearly enough to send her racing back to her rooms, if George had not placed his hand atop her own, under the guise of guiding her to the ballroom, to prevent it.

Once again, she found herself wishing that she could live in this lone moment forever. The harsh realities of her real life seemed another world from that which she had lived in the recent weeks. She could almost convince herself that all the danger had passed, that this was far enough from Jasper to escape his notice and start anew.

Still, it would not do.

Whether she cared to admit it or not, there was still risk that someone might bring word to the earl of her whereabouts. Even if that dreaded moment never came to pass, her dream could never be for no matter what else happened, she was already married.

This fantasy that she had created, she now realized, centered on the delusion that she might one day be able to build a future with George and Marietta. A real future, a life. It had been amplified by the arrival of her moon's blood the week prior, finally confirming the truth that Jasper had not got her with child despite his best efforts. The truth that she was in love with Lord Halthaven.

She had grown to love his caring heart and the steady nature of his character. The dream of a quiet life together was never going to come to pass and she needed to come to terms with that knowledge. However, a heart is not as easy to convince as the mind, so when the music started up and Lord Halthaven swept her onto the dance floor,

Prudence could not help but give herself over to the dream for just this one night.

Tomorrow, she would be gone to whatever end of the earth the Mother Abbess had secured in a valiant attempt to keep her hidden. What harm could come from allowing herself one small moment of pleasure, one which she might look back upon and treasure for the rest of her days?

The music galloped along at a lively pace, leaving the dancers winded and laughing from the exertion. There was nothing of romance about the tune, but Prudence enjoyed herself all the more for its energetic rumble. She could feel a hundred eyes upon her as they whispered and wondered about her identity.

She allowed a giggle to bubble up from within as the fun of the game took her over. She was neither the most enchanting, nor most beautiful, lady in attendance. Nor did she wish to be. Yet, neither was she overlooked as she had come to expect.

It was a boon to her confidence to know that, as her own person, she might still have value in this fickle world. Perhaps the small neighborhood of Nettlefold had been too limited in its scope. Perhaps she had limited herself with her own assumptions about her value, or lack thereof.

This evening, she determined, would be the birth of a new Prudence. Nevermore would she look down upon herself for the amusement of others. She would surround herself only with those that brought light and happiness to her world.

How she wished, more than anything, that she might not have to leave in the morning.

She had not realized that she had spoken the words aloud until her gaze met with the warmth of her partner and she saw that very wish reflected in his eyes. Before he could reply, she turned her head and made a comment about the size of the crowd or some other such nonsense.

George had the grace not to press the topic, for it could only end in sadness for the both of them. Still, she felt his arm tighten at her back as he pulled her just a hair closer. She wondered if he too was doing his best to savor what few moments remained in their short acquaintance.

The set ended and in her flustered state, Prudence decided to return to her rooms for the remainder of the evening. Just as she turned to leave, she felt a slight pressure upon her hand, the softest of touches that would have barely been noticed had it not shot straight to her heart.

"Promise me the waltz," George begged with a regretful voice.

He was loathe to return to his duties and take his leave from her side, but the promise of another dance, a waltz at that, seemed to fortify his spirit. Prudence could not deny him the pleasure. Besides, there was nothing more that she desired than to be swept along upon his arm in the risqué twirl of the dance. She would remain rooted in this very spot until he returned if he asked it. She gave the slightest of nods and felt his fingers feather against hers once more.

How was it that such a soft caress, too small to even

be noticed by a prying eye, could cause her heart to race and thump as if it were trying to burst from her chest? Her head spun like a drunkard and her eyes could not help but follow him as he made his way through the crowd to the far side of the room to greet his guests.

All of Jasper's pressure and forcefulness had been revolting. There had been nothing gentle about him and therefore he had elicited no desire from his wife. Yet, Lord Halthaven had barely brushed against her, held her in his arms only once for a dance, and never made any overt gesture toward her body.

Despite her assumptions that men turned into beasts after the chase was over and they had a woman alone, Prudence felt certain that it would not be so with George. To be loved and cared for with such tenderhearted kindness was better than any dream and yet, she could not accept his affections.

What a terrible joke The Lord in Heaven had played upon her heart, to let her encounter such a man when it was already too late.

She wandered aimlessly through the crowd for a few hours, playing the role of distant cousin. She accepted a glass of liquored punch from a friendly young gentleman named Max, who declared himself the baron's oldest school chum, and went on and on about George's fine character.

The drink, and the company, allowed her to relax. She even allowed Max to partner her for two dances in a row, which would have been scandalous if it had not been for his own wife laughing along upon the arm of George at their side.

The foursome completed a quadrille, which allowed Prudence a few stolen passes with the gentleman of her choice. Never had she enjoyed a ball so much as this evening. When he returned to his duties, she found herself enjoying her time with George's friends. It was easy because she still had the waltz to look forward to.

When the first notes of the waltz began a short while later, Lord Halthaven was nowhere to be found. Prudence could not help but feel her shoulders droop in disappointment. The evening was almost over and she would miss the part that she had most looked forward to.

Then, like a rush of fresh air, he sped past from behind her, grasping her hand and pulling her along after him as they raced toward the floor. Prudence laughed with glee at the carefree and childish manner that she had never once before felt bold enough to risk.

"Come now, we're late," he said with panting breath as he drew her into his arms.

She threw her head back and laughed with abandon. It felt good to give in to the moment, if only for just this once.

13

*J*asper Numbton dipped his head low to conceal the snarl that had transformed his features from that of a jovial new acquaintance and revealed the demon that dwelled within. He had secured invitation to the Harvest Ball by having let a nearby summer house of a distant acquaintance who had returned to London for the coming winter.

A false name and the growth of neatly trimmed facial hair were enough to conceal the truth of his identity from any but those who knew him well. All of the neighborhood had been invited and so Jasper had decided to make his appearance to see if word of his wife might be found in such a crowd.

Perry waited outside, plying the drivers with drink and picking their memories for mention of a buxom lady traveling alone. When Jasper had discovered that the eldest Baggington had joined the nearby convent, it occurred to him that Prudence might have stopped here.

Never had he expected that she might be in attendance. Nor that she was a clear favorite to the host, who raced away from their introductions as soon as was proper to sweep Prudence onto the dance floor for the waltz.

It was brazen! It was an outrage! Prudence was his! Had the little harlot been dancing without care all these weeks, never once concerned that Jasper might hunt her down? He was determined to out her, ruin her, take her home and beat her for her disobedience.

No, he calmed himself with a series of long, slow breaths. He must remain cool and collected. Too often rage might spoil a plot for those who were not as brilliant and cunning as himself. Lord Fondleton never allowed his emotions to take over his plotting. It was for that reason that he was so very successful in his exploits.

Except, he thought, for that one time in Nettlefold... and all knew how *that* had turned out. If it were not for that very slip-up he would not be chasing after *the Baggage* and he might have had the pleasure of the fine, Juliana instead. How the lovely Juliana had escaped him, Jasper could not say, but some small part of him still blamed Prudence for that failure.

He cursed the woman. She was neither beautiful, nor interesting enough to warrant this much effort. Still, his reputation would be in shambles if it became known that his wife, and a homely one at that, had run away. And now that she would make a cuckold of him with some back country baron! The rage near overtook him.

Lord Fondleton chose a shaded corner from which to watch the couple upon the floor. Prudence looked different than he remembered. Less showy and, somehow for that, more appealing. It was as if a light had lit from within her and he felt all at once possessive.

How dare she hang upon the arm of that gentleman and stare up at him with an unobstructed smile? She ought to have been *honored* that he had taken her as his wife, forced or not. Any woman was fortunate to have his affections and he would not be put to shame by some do-gooder named Halthaven!

Of course he had heard all about Lord Halthaven. He was a private gentleman with impeccable standing in the community and a reputation of charitable endeavors. He had a charge, Jasper recalled, the young waif that was peering through the rail from above at the entrance. Why would such a man entangle himself in the complexities that was an affair with a married woman?

Perhaps it was all a show and he was really molten-hearted. Had not Jasper himself done his best to keep up appearances so that all questions would be firmly absolved? He doubted it. This Lord Halthaven was all too pure and well-liked to be a blackguard. No, he must have been fooled by the witch. Perhaps she had appealed to his bleeding heart.

It made him sick to think of it. What a boring lifestyle this man must live. It was a shame really, Jasper thought, that he would waste away in this dark wood and never explore the pleasures of life that were like low-hung fruit, ready for the picking by any peer who wished a taste.

Prudence laughed as she whirled by.

Oh, how Jasper wished to jump out and reveal himself. The look on her face would be worth a thousand moments of pleasure as she crumbled before him. Yet, he did not move. As an observer of people, he wished to know more about this gallant host who seemed so taken with Jasper's own harlot wife.

He was rather proud of the wench. Never had he expected her to be so bold as to search for attentions elsewhere, so soon after having slipped away in the depths of night. Wherever had she gotten this rogue confidence? It made him hungry to have her again, if only to watch the light dim from her eyes as she became docile once more under his hand. That was his favorite part, their submission.

Knowing that he had won, that he would always win, was more gratifying than any word of praise that fell from a woman's blasphemous lips. He'd rather they not speak at all. Perhaps when he got her home he would bid her silence for the next month or two. She did not need to speak to breed his heir.

He slipped the flask from his pocket and took a hearty drag on the liquor. The burn in his throat brought his muscles to life and his mind into focus on the task at hand. Like a beast on the prowl he looked upon his unsuspecting prey.

She never once looked his way. Her eyes were only for the baron. Jasper's blood boiled as his mind called out for her to feel his presence, to writhe with fear that he was near. She took no note. Instead, she continued to laugh and smile as if nothing were amiss. As if nothing ever had been, or would ever be again.

Her hair trailed down her back in the bland colored ringlets that he vaguely recalled. Except, the front portions were piled atop her head in a somewhat pleasing way, as if she had suddenly discovered the proper technique to play up her features.

Gone were the garish gowns and potent perfumes that she had brought by the trunkful. Even her voice sounded different when she passed by in her conversation with the baron. It was lower, sultry and appealing. Had she changed so much in so few weeks?

Another swig of liquid fire flowed from his mouth to his gut, emboldening his passions and inciting his anger.

"Oh, Prudence," he muttered to himself. "How far you shall fall."

The music came to an end. He watched as the couple lingered at the center of the floor for a moment too long, as if they did not wish to part. It was shameless, really.

How dare she entertain the attentions of another man when she belonged to him? A lesser man, at that. Why choose a baron when you could have an earl?

Prudence appeared flushed as she thanked the gentleman for the dance with a nod and a slight curtsy. He looked as if he were about to speak when she turned upon her heel and raced from the room. Lord Halthaven might have followed after her if he had not been waylaid by a guest who maneuvered him into the next dance with her pockmarked daughter.

Jasper could not help but laugh as he slunk after his wife and left another gentleman to partner the wretch. Even Prudence was better than that thing.

He stepped out into the main hall just in time to see a

flash of Prudence's gown slip out between a pair of large glass doors that led onto the veranda. He peeked up at the rail of the stair to see if the little pair of eyes followed his movements, but all that remained to be seen was the tail of a plait that had fallen through the bars.

The child must have drifted off to sleep. All the better, Jasper thought. There would be none to witness his approach upon his unsuspecting wife.

She had made her way to the edge of the veranda and was looking out upon the grounds as the moon shone through a misty fog. Lord Fondleton kept to the shadows as he plotted his reveal. He took his time, measuring each step so that no sound fell in the quiet of the night.

It was a painstaking process, but he did not wish her to know of his presence until it was too late and he was upon her. Each patient step brought him nearer to his prize. He could not help but thrill at the prospect of her fear, her agony as he shattered this dream world that she had created.

Then, from a second pair of doors between them, a figure stepped out into the darkness and approached the traitorous woman. Jasper slipped behind a potted palm and crouched low so as not to be seen. He was not near enough to hear their words, but he could see all that occurred by the light of the moon. Again, he suppressed a bestial snarl.

14

*P*rudence stood at the rail and looked down upon the well-manicured grass. A ghostly layer of fog was beginning to brew. Rather than cause her to shiver, however, she found it quite beautiful as it moved between the trees and over the rolling hills.

"Prudence?" A voice at her side asked with concern. "What are you doing out here? You'll catch your death."

"Hello, George. I only wished for some fresh air," she replied to Lord Halthaven as he stepped out onto the veranda.

"Have you found it?" he asked with a laugh.

"Crisper air there has never been," she confirmed. He offered her a shawl that he had grabbed from the rack in the study as he had passed through. She allowed him to drape it over her shoulders though she was quick to pull away.

"You oughtn't to be out here alone."

"I know that," she said with a sigh. "I only wanted a moment."

"I apologize," he bowed his head with sincerity, "I did not mean to intrude. It was only... when you raced away..." He shook his head as if unsure how to complete the thought.

Prudence took a deep breath and released it slowly. The action did little to calm her racing nerves.

"I..." she too seemed to have tied her tongue. "I leave in the morning," she offered as a lame sort of excuse.

"I know," he murmured. "I wish it were not so."

"Don't say such things," Prudence cried.

"Why not? Would you rather I pretend otherwise?"

"I do not know," she shook her head. She was flustered and nervous. She wanted him to leave so that she might feel less of an ache in her heart and yet she worried that if he did it would grow worse still.

"Halthaven Manor has been brighter for your presence," he argued. "I've never been happier than when I am with you."

"It cannot be..." she said in a whisper as she turned away. A soft hand upon her chin brought her back to look upon the warmth of his features. That gentle gesture, more than anything caused the crack in her heart to deepen.

"What cannot be?" he asked. His breath was warm, his mouth a mere inch from her own trembling lips.

"This..." she sighed. Even to her own ears she could hear the longing that betrayed her denial.

Against her will, her eyes fluttered closed. If he would kiss her she would be powerless to stop it. If she were being truthful, she wanted him to. She wanted to know what it was like to be kissed with gentle love just once.

Rather than the pressure of his lips, she felt his forehead come to rest against her own. His breath shook with the frustration of restraint.

"Stay."

His words were neither command, nor question. She could feel the yearning of his heart and she wished more than anything that she could lean into it and accept. How cruel a world this must be to find such a love and not be able to accept it. To be forbidden to accept it.

"I cannot." Her words hitched in her throat. A tear rolled down her cheek and Lord Halthaven brushed it away before it could fall from the proud line of her chin.

"I can protect you," he promised. "I would do anything to protect you."

"I know that," she cried. "I believe that with all of my heart."

"Then what is it?" he asked.

The words of the Mother Abbess swirled through her mind, warning against revealing any detail of her former life, particularly anything pertaining to the Earl of Fondleton. She dared not put Lord Halthaven at risk with knowledge that should be protected at all costs. It was not his burden to bear.

Prudence reached her hand up and cupped the cheek of the man that she loved. How was she to push him away without destroying both of their hearts?

"You are too kind," she whispered. "If there were another way... but there is not." She shook her head. His hand was atop her own and his thumb stroked a soothing pattern against her skin. The sensation sent a tingle of pleasure through her body. Again, she considered turning her mouth up to press her lips against his.

"I love you," he replied.

At first, she thought that she had misheard him. When she looked up into his eyes she knew that her ears had not failed her. He loved her! Oh, how she wished to throw herself into his arms and accept his affection. She loved him too.

She wanted to say the words, but they stuck in her throat. The image of Jasper crossed her mind, and a wave of fear and disgust overtook her. The moment was shattered by the memory of truth. This love, this life, could never be.

"Let us not make things more complicated than they already are," she said with a groan of agony.

Still, she leaned into his frame, allowing him to wrap his arms around her waist and provide the comfort that she so desperately needed. Never before had she been held such by a gentleman. She closed her eyes and settled her cheek to his shoulder.

"Why must it be complicated?" he said with a laugh of frustration. "This all seems so simple and right."

She nodded against him. She could feel the warmth of his skin through the silk of his waistcoat, smell the scent of him and hear the beat of his heart in her ear.

A flash of movement in the shadows at the far end of the veranda caught her attention. By the time she turned to look more fully, the figure was out of sight. She might have imagined it. Her mind seemed determined to play all sorts of tricks on her nowadays.

"I thought..." she raised her head and looked into the distance. "I thought I saw something." She shook her head. "It was just a trick of the light."

"Let me ease your worries." He braced his hands upon her shoulders and allowed his fingers to trail down her arms until their hands folded together. "Allow me to carry your burdens."

He could sense her unease and she wanted nothing more than to lay her troubles at his feet. It was unfair of her to wish such things, when there was naught that could be done to free her from her lifelong commitment. One might turn heads with the suggestion of an annulment, but never would such a prospect be permitted in her case. Jasper, for certain, would never agree.

"I love you," he repeated. This time, he ensured that she was looking full into his eyes when he spoke the words, so that there could be no doubt.

"I love you too," she gasped and the tears began to flow freely. "But it cannot be."

"Why?" he demanded. She could see the hopeless frustration upon his features as he fought a battle against some invisible barrier.

"Please," she begged. "You must understand. I cannot..."

George feathered his fingers through the curls of her lengthy hair until her sobbing subsided. He said not another word, knowing that it would only cause her more distress. Instead, he held her in his arms as they both pondered their impending farewell.

"I should retire. The hour is late." She shifted as if to

pull away, but it was a half-hearted effort as her hands still clung to his lapel.

"I'd rather savor our last moments, if I must watch you leave." He offered a shy smile. The music could still be heard from the distant ballroom where his guests were being neglected. Neither cared. Soon enough the ballroom would empty, and the manor would feel as empty as Prudence's aching heart.

"No," she argued. "It would be best if we say no more. Then we shall have nothing to look back upon... and wonder."

"You lie to yourself," he laughed. "We shall always wonder either way." He was so close, his breath upon her cheek. She could not deny the truth of his words. She could not even think. His nearness was robbing her of her wits.

"I would rather know, than wonder," he said. With that, he kissed her with a gentle passion that pooled through her body like a hot tea on a cold day.

She could not even feign resistance. Prudence gave in at once and threw her arms about his neck as she clung to him in an attempt to control the trembling of her body. She opened her mouth to him and allowed the kiss to deepen. It was unlike anything that she had ever experienced. They kissed with the urgency that could only come from the knowledge that, come the morrow, they would part forever.

With that thought, she clung to him, as if she would never let go. Though she knew it was wrong, Prudence threw herself into the moment. If she could shower Lord Halthaven with her love for just this one moment, then she wanted there to be no doubt as to the depth of her feeling. For just this moment, she could imagine she was his.

The sound of a whip cracking and a carriage taking off toward the wood brought them to their senses. In the distance, they could see a covered carriage rolling away at a leisurely pace. Guests were beginning to leave and, though they had not been happened upon, it was only a matter of moments before someone would come looking.

They could not risk being discovered. People could not scrutinize her alias too closely. She could not bring such censure down upon George, not with all he had done for her. She let her fingers caress his cheek as if she could remember every curve of it, the high cheekbones and his full lips. She let her hand drop to her side. Prudence took a step back and dipped into a low, shaking curtsy, at last taking her eyes from his.

"Good evening, my lord," she stammered.

Before Lord Halthaven could reach out to stop her, she turned upon her heel and raced toward the hall from whence she had come. Just as she rounded the corner, Mr. Perkins stepped into the hall. He had been searching for his master in the ballroom and come up empty handed.

"Miss Riverford!" he said with surprise. "You look as if you've seen a ghost."

"Not at all," she pressed her hands to her flushed cheeks. "I was only looking for Marietta," she lied.

"Mrs. Perkins tucked her in not a quarter hour passed," he said with a nod. "She fell asleep at the top of the stair and would have awoken with an awful crick in her neck had she not been moved."

"Right then," Prudence blew out a breath and hurried past him. "Off to bed for me as well. Goodnight, Mr. Perkins."

"Goodnight, Miss Riverford," he replied.

With that, she rushed up the stairs before the butler could say another word. She hoped that Lord Halthaven had returned to the ballroom through his study so that their might be no suspicion of them having been together. He was too careful to risk a rumor to her name, so she refused to allow herself to dwell upon it.

Her mind was too full of the memory of their embrace to think of much else. She let her fingers trace her lips, thinking of his kiss. She could still feel the heat of his hands upon her arms. She knew that she had a long, sleepless night ahead of her. If she could drift off, her dreams would be filled with the promise of love that would never come to pass. A pleasure and a nightmare all at once.

She locked the door to her chamber and without calling a maid to undress she slipped beneath the covers to cry herself dry. What a cruel, cruel world it had turned out to be, she thought. But she had always known the world was cruel. She had only escaped it these past few months.

15

a soft knock on her door woke Prudence from her slumber. She rolled from the coverlet, which had entangled her like some clinging octopus in the long hours of the night. Her hair was awry and her gown mussed but she opened the door a crack to reveal the tired face of Mrs. Perkins.

"A letter for you, Miss," she said with a yawn. "It just arrived by special courier."

The folded envelope was slipped through the door as the housekeeper straightened her cap and slipped back off to her room.

Prudence turned the mail in her hand to discover the wax seal which caused her heart to thump as if it were to escape from the confines of her breast. The Fondleton crest stared back at her, emblazoned in red.

She gasped and dropped the letter, her hand covering the scream that threatened to escape her lips.

He had found her.

With trembling fingers she bent to pick up the letter. She peeled it open with care, fearful that it might somehow cause her harm in doing so. That was ridiculous, she thought. Of course it was only a letter. Yet, it felt like a snake poised for the strike. Venom dripping from its contents.

The truth was not far off. Lord Fondleton's correspondence dealt nothing less than a fatal blow to his wife's heart.

Marietta had been taken.

The demand was that Prudence appear for her exchange in person, alone. Only then would the girl remain unharmed, and untouched.

She cursed the rogue and his terrible plots. Of course Fondleton would think this was some sort of game. How many hours had the frightened girl been wracked with worry and fear for her own life?

The letter gave express instructions that Prudence arrive alone and no alert be given to any in the household. She knew not how he would monitor that detail, but she had no doubt that he was more than capable of setting some paid crony to watch the manor.

Prudence cursed herself that she had not checked on the child before she retired to her own rooms. She had been too distraught over her impending departure, as well as her romantic encounter with Lord Halthaven. Her departure would have to wait, she thought. It would be impossible for her to leave knowing that the child was in danger in her stead. If any harm came to Marietta she would never forgive herself. She was sure that Jasper was counting on that resolve to stay her lips. She had sworn to protect the girl and now because of Prudence she was in danger, within the clutches of her vile husband.

Prudence would adhere to his demands, with one exception. She would leave a letter for Lord Halthaven that explained that Marietta was missing and that she had gone to her retrieval. No more, no less. Then, when the gentleman woke, he might look for the girl if, for any reason, Prudence was unsuccessful in her attempt.

She packed her small carpet bag and made for the door. Only afterward did it occur to her that the small, fragile Posey, who had already once escaped the wrath of Lord Fondleton, had been in Marietta's room last night as well. She slipped down the hall to the girl's room, where her disappearance had yet to be noticed.

Prudence wished that she could wake the entire house, but she knew her husband well enough to take his word to heart. If he suspected that an alarm had been raised he would harm the girl without hesitation. She knew better than any what he was capable of.

A scuffling sound came from beneath the bed as soon as she stepped into the room. Posey bounded out from under the ruffled bed skirt. The poor creature hopped upon three legs, holding one injured paw in the air as she went.

Prudence cursed Lord Fondleton under her breath and scooped the dog into her arms. Posey whimpered and licked her wound. The rascal must have kicked her or some other such atrocity, Prudence determined with a scowl. She soothed the animal and then settled her upon a blanket on the floor, so that she might not injure herself further by leaping from the bed. Someone would come for the pup, she thought. It would not do for Prudence to bring the dog with her. Far be it from Jasper Numbton to preserve the life of an innocent animal.

On silent footsteps, she crept from the house. It would not take long to walk across the fields to the neighboring estate, where Jasper had claimed to have taken residence. Only a few months ago, his words would have had her obeying without hesitation; now she attempted to skirt his demands as best as possible without his knowledge. Once Lord Halthaven discovered the note, she knew that he would act with discretion.

Her walk across the fields was a lonely one. The first rays of sun had yet to creep over the tops of the trees. The world had yet to come alive for the day and all seemed silent save for the snap of twigs and grasses beneath her feet as she picked her way toward her demise.

The neighboring estate seemed friendly enough, except for the bleak darkness of its windows. Despite the call for her arrival, there was not a single light that was lit within the manor. A shadow stepped out from the edge of the garden just as she entered the property.

Jasper.

"Darling," he said with a snarl. "How I have missed you."

She did not believe a word of it. In fact, he seemed all too pleased with himself and the prospect of her suffering to be taken at his word.

All she offered in response was a hardened glare.

He leered at her and laughed. His hand lifted and struck her cheek faster than the blink of an eye. The skin smarted and she knew that she would have a bruise that would cover most of the right half of her face. Already, her eye seemed determined to remain closed from the pain of it. She refused to show him her fear and so she stood tall all the same. Her response seemed to infuriate him as he struck her again, this time splitting the skin upon her brow.

His fingers wrapped around her arm and she cried out in pain.

"Jasper, please," she gasped. "Set Marietta free."

"Oh, shall I?" he laughed. "At first, I might have, but once I saw what a shameless hussy you have become I knew that I must make your man suffer as well."

"What are you talking about?" She feigned innocence.

"He'll come for you," Jasper glowered.

"No, he won't," she cried. Again, his fingers twisted the skin upon her arm and she sunk to her knees as she begged for mercy.

"He will," Jasper spat, "and he shall suffer as well."

"He doesn't know where I am. I told no one just as you asked," she pleaded. "He won't come. Please release the child."

Jasper hummed as he considered her words. He seemed bolstered by the knowledge that she might have followed his instruction. There was nothing that pleased Lord Fondleton more than feeling like he was in control.

He began to drag her toward the stables. She stumbled along beside him, her bag long forgotten at the edge of the wood. Her only thought was that she needed to ensure that Marietta was set free. Do what he may to her, Prudence would endure. She only wished for Marietta's safety.

"I honestly did not expect to find you here," Jasper continued. "What sort of mindless fool goes to their only relation who has moved away? It was too simple, really. I wonder why I didn't think of it from the start. I suppose I expected that you might have more sense than that. It appears that I was wrong."

Prudence remained silent as he slung insults at her, one after the other.

"Where are the clothes that you wore last evening?" he asked. "This scrap of garbage is not fit for a pauper. At least last night you had some minor appeal."

Prudence did not care what he thought of her attire. She was dressed in the plain grey frock from the abbey, for she had not wished to make her departure in any of the fine clothes that Lizzie had made for her.

"You were there?" she gasped before she could stop herself.

"Of course I was there," Jasper growled. "I saw you, prancing about like the harlot I know you are. Hanging upon your gentleman, really? Are you so easy as to throw yourself at any man with a title? A baron at that? One who lives in a hovel of a manor in the middle of this godforsaken forest?" Lord Fondleton shivered as if the very thought was repulsive. "Perhaps if you put half as much effort toward me I might find you the least bit appealing. We shall need to work on that. As it is, I think you'll do well to be locked away. Your meals shall be brought to you, and your clothes...well I don't see that you will need any."

"You bastard," she spat.

"Female melancholy is a truly terrible disease." He laughed his evil laugh and Prudence did not even deign to answer. Of course he had spied on her. She should have known that on the best night of her life Jasper would have been there to hang a black sheath over even its memory.

As they entered the barn a muffled cry from the back stall had Prudence jerking her arm free of her husband's grasp and racing toward the terrified child. Jasper followed behind at a casual pace, as if he were not the least concerned about the state of things.

Prudence took note of Perry, Lord Fondleton's henchman as she pushed her way into the stall. Of course he would come with extra muscle on hand.

Marietta was curled in the corner with her hands and feet tied and her mouth gagged with a soiled cloth. Prudence's hands worked like a horse on the wind as she freed the girl from her confines. Still, the latch of the stall door clicked shut behind her, and she knew that they were trapped. It was no matter, she crooned to the child. They were together. She would protect Marietta.

"Your face!" Marietta exclaimed as soon as she was set free and Prudence removed her gag. She wrapped her tiny arms around Prudence and buried her head in her neck.

"It is nothing," Prudence whispered. "Marietta, you must tell me true. Have they harmed you in any way?"

"Other than causing a me a fright and binding my limbs..." Marietta shook her head. "No. Though my mind was filled with all sorts of terrible things. I thought for sure I'd be killed."

Prudence brushed her hands over the girl's forehead and whispered promises that she would do all in her power to set Marietta free.

"Who are they?" the girl whispered. "What sort of terrible man would do such a thing?"

"Shut up in there!" Perry's voice came from over the wall. "Another word and I'll give you a wholloping."

"You have permission to do so, such as you please as long as the ladies are fit to ride," Lord Fondleton's voice chimed in a cheerful cantor. "I'll be in town for a short while to get the last of our supplies," he informed the man in a whisper. Prudence strained her ears to hear each word. "We shall be off before the full sun. I expect the horses ready and the ladies tied before my return. We shall take them both I think, just to be sure that Lord Halthaven knows to keep his filthy hands off of my wife."

Marietta gasped at the final word and Prudence hushed her before the sound escaped her lips.

"My lady," Jasper's mocking face peered over the edge of the stall and down upon the cowering women. "I am pleased by your willing return. Perhaps, for that, I shall lessen your punishment."

"I hope you rot," Prudence spat. Now that she knew that he had no intention of releasing Marietta, she had no intention of complying with any of his demands.

"Oh, it is too late to strike an iron now," he laughed. "Though, I cannot deny that I find your spirit most amusing. Perhaps your spawn will be just as lively."

Prudence screamed a very unladylike insult and

threw a handful of crisp straw ineffectually in his direction. The stalks fluttered down in the air between them, never having reached the full length of their intended destination. Lord Fondleton laughed all the more for her effort.

They listened as he walked away. It was not until the door to the barn swung shut that Marietta allowed herself to give in to her fear and sob into Prudence's skirts.

"What are we to do?" she whispered. Prudence hushed her once more.

Perry was still standing guard outside of the stall, though he seemed more interested in the bottle of wine that he was uncorking to pour down his gullet.

"Are you truly a lady?" Marietta asked with awe.

"Yes," Prudence replied. "That pile of scum that just left was Jasper, the Earl of Fondleton, and my husband by unfortunate mishap."

"Did you ever love him?" Marietta's eyes were wide. It was clear that her mind had clung to the thought that there might be something between Prudence and Lord Halthaven. Jasper's outburst had even confirmed as much.

"Could anyone?" Prudence said sadly. "I had once hoped that he was a decent man, but I should have known better from the off. I do not believe Jasper Numbton has a kind bone in his body."

"Me either," Marietta confirmed. "He kicked Posey and threatened to shoot her if I didn't come quietly."

The girl buried her face in her hands and cried anew.

"Posey is fine," Prudence assured her. "Her paw is

injured, but I am certain that she will heal up in time. Right now we need to focus on getting you out of here and back to George so that he can protect you."

"What of you?" Marietta asked, unsatisfied with the answer.

"My future is set," she replied with a resigned sigh. "Lord Fondleton is my husband. I am bound to him whether I wish it or no. It is for your safety that I am concerned. I shall be fine; I promise you."

"No, you won't," the girl argued with wisdom beyond her years. "Look at your eye! He has darkened your daylights. He'll kill you as soon as keep you!"

"Don't you fret," Prudence tucked Marietta's hair behind her ear and did her best to put on a brave face. "I can deal with him. It is you I wish to keep from harm."

Marietta threw her arms around her companion's neck once more and pressed a kiss to her cheek.

"I'll be brave if you will," the child said with a nod. Prudence agreed though, to herself, she thought that Marietta was thankfully for the moment unharmed. Perhaps the innocence of her mind might be preserved with quick action.

Prudence thought that if they could just wait long enough for Perry to be well into his bottle, they might stand a chance of convincing him to let Marietta out to relieve herself. Then, the girl could make a run for it. She was fast, for a small thing, and could easily outrun the drunken blundering fool.

Prudence did not want to think about the consequences of such a risky action, but she cared not. Her main concern was that Lord Fondleton might return before Perry had reached the point of inebriation in which he could be manipulated. Prudence remembered that the man was quick to his drink and would not stop until his words slurred and his feet fell out from beneath him. She hoped to play upon that habit if at all possible.

16

*T*he minutes ticked by at an agonizing pace. When the drunkard began to laugh and speak to himself, Prudence knew that it was time to enact her plan. She whispered into Marietta's ear the instruction and, though the girl seemed loathe to leave her, she gave a firm scowl and demanded that she must be obeyed.

"You run straight home, fast as you can and don't look back for anything," she hissed. "Find George and tell him that I went away. Can you do that?"

"He won't believe me," Marietta argued. "He shall come after you."

"You mustn't allow it," Prudence pressed. "Tell him I returned to my husband, if you must. He'll be hurt but free of danger."

"You can't go with that monster!"

"Hush now!" Prudence scolded. "You must do as I say and all will be well. Lord Halthaven will keep you safe. That is all that matters."

"I want you to come home with me, with us!" Marietta cried.

Perry heard her tears and shouted that the ladies remain silent. Prudence gave Marietta a firm look to silence her objections.

"She is in need of relief," Prudence called to the slow fool. "You've kept her here all night without it and a poor captor you've turned out to be."

"Piss in the stall," Perry said.

"She cannot," Prudence replied. "I should have known you know nothing."

"Shut up, woman!" Perry shouted.

"She's a child," Prudence replied in kind. "Unless a mere child is too much for you to handle…"

The door to the stall was yanked open and Prudence leapt back in fear. Perry's glowering face was shoved through the opening. His breath stank of wine and his eyes shifted between the females.

"You!" he jabbed a finger toward Prudence. "You stay here. She can go, but I swear if there's any funny business Lord Fondleton won't be happy. You know how he gets…" The leer in his eyes told her that he was looking forward to her punishments.

"I do," Prudence said with a proud nod. "She shall be only a short while and then return."

Marietta nodded in agreement, but her feet were restless upon the ground. Like a filly upon new legs she was preparing to test the strength of her muscles as she ran as fast as her growing frame would permit.

"I'll skin ya alive if ya aren't back in a blink, do ya hear me?" he breathed into Marietta's face. "You don't want the lady here to suffer for it. I've seen m'lord break her skin more times than I can count and I can assure you he'll break more than skin this time."

Marietta's eyes grew wide with fear and she trembled with uncertainty.

"She understands," Prudence replied, pushing the girl from the stall so that she might not change her mind. The door slammed shut between them and Prudence heard one small whimper before Marietta followed the slovenly servant from the stables.

A moment later, she heard a masculine cry of pain as if Marietta had kicked her oppressor. Perry shouted and cursed, but it was clear that he was in no state to race after the young girl. Prudence felt the fear settle upon her. She was relieved that Marietta was free, but afraid of what might come in reply.

Perry stormed back into the stables and ripped the door to the stall open.

"You lying wench!" he growled. "SHE BOLTED!"

He reached forward and grabbed Prudence by the front of her dress until she was forced to raise to her toes lest he choke her with it.

One sharp shove had her back slamming against the wall. She cried out in pain, unable to contain the sound as the air was thrust from her lungs.

"I'll kill you myself," he slurred. He raised his fist between them so she might see his intent.

She closed her eyes in anticipation of the blow. One eye was already swollen shut, what need had she for the other at this point?

Rather than his fist landing upon her face, she was jerked forward by some unforeseen force.

She landed upon her knees amongst the straw. When she opened her eyes, Perry was lying unconscious on the floor beside her with a dark figure standing between them. The figure turned around and Prudence looked up to see none other than Lord Halthaven standing above her. When he had jerked Perry from behind, she had been pulled forward by the fiend's firm grasp.

Prudence scampered to her feet and gaped open-mouthed at her savior.

"How did you know where to find me?" she stammered. Marietta had only just made her escape. She could not have sent for help so soon. She realized at once that his primary concern would be the girl. "Marietta escaped," she explained before he could ask the question. "How is it that you are here?"

"I knew where to ask the right questions," he explained.

"You ought to have come to us first," Temperance said as she stepped out from behind Lord Halthaven with a look of shock and relief upon her face. "This is the only estate that is let for the winter and the abbey keeps track of the tenancy. Reverend Mother knew at once that you must be here when Lord Halthaven said that you had left on foot. We came straight away."

Prudence tried to explain that she had been too flustered in the moment to do anything, but solve the situation as instructed. Even her note had been hurried and vague. George and Temperance excused her mishap by expressing their pleasure that she, and Marietta, were safe in the end.

"A touching sentiment," a cool voice came from the aisle.

The trio turned to look down the barrel of a gun that was pointed straight at Lord Halthaven's chest.

"Miss Baggington," Jasper said with approval as his eyes traveled up and down Temperance's slender form. "What a perfect waste of flesh, in my opinion, that you should commit yourself to celibacy. It appears that I've got myself the least of the Baggington sisters. My, but if I could have had you..."

Temperance's lip curled in disgust.

"How dare you speak that way to a lady," Lord Halthaven admonished, as he positioned himself to block both of the sisters from Lord Fondleton's disgusting gaze.

"Are you referring to my whore of a wife, or her exquisite sister?" Jasper added without hesitation. He enjoyed the game and seemed to be reveling in the excitement.

"Both," Lord Halthaven hissed. He seemed slightly caught off guard by the mention of Prudence as Lord Fondleton's wife, but he recovered quickly.

"Ah, I see you were unaware that Prudence is mine," Jasper pressed the barb further. With each verbal blow his grin widened. "I am afraid she was forced upon me. Faithless as she may be, she is still my property, and I will have her."

"My father will kill you when he finds out how you've treated her!" Temperance shouted.

"Ha!" Lord Fondleton laughed. "As if that vile creature

would have any right to criticize me! Not, after he had his turn with her." Fondleton shook his head in mock disgust. "His own daughter, can you imagine."

Prudence felt as though she had been struck. She stood frozen with horror as her deepest secrets and failures were laid forth before the man that she loved.

"I noticed my wife's deficiency at once. She'd been tainted and ruined long before me. She will give no man satisfaction, of that I am certain. There is no pleasure left in her."

"No matter Father's sins, he will have you hung when word gets out of your misdeeds." The eldest Baggington seemed to have found her voice. Temperance looked down her petite nose at their assailant, as if he were no more than a worm beneath her shoe.

Jasper snarled in response. His hatred that he should be treated as lesser than any man was his greatest weakness. Temperance had honed in on that knowledge from the first. In defense of her sister she would pretend that they had a protector on their side, though both sisters doubted their father cared what really happened to either of them.

"Too bad he's dead." Lord Fondleton delivered the final blow with a peeling laughter. "Oh, you didn't know?" He moved his pistol in a lazy circle as he relished the telling of his tale.

Prudence could not believe his words. Could her father truly be dead?

Fondleton grinned. His pleasure was too great. It had to be true.

"He died not three weeks past, some illness or other

that came on without warning. Died in his sleep, I heard. The funeral was small, no one liked him much anyway. I attended on behalf of my poor wife, who was too ill to appear herself."

Prudence realized that Jasper had already been spreading the tales that would permit him to keep her locked away for the rest of her days. If a woman was too ill to attend her own father's funeral, then no one would dare to question why she had missed any other more frivolous excursion.

"You fiend!" Prudence replied. "You've no right to toy with people. Just leave me be and we can both be on our way! Say I died, I don't care! Wouldn't you prefer to start anew?"

"Our marriage offers no limits to my... encounters." Jasper laughed once more. "I may have whom I want when I want them. Why should I allow you freedom when it is much more satisfying to have a kept woman? Besides, I need a legitimate heir to prevent any bastard claims from holding sway over my fortunes. It's a pity that you seem without child at the moment. I had hoped when you ran that it meant I had succeeded thus far."

Prudence watched the hard line of George's jaw clench and his fists ball at his sides. Had it not been for the weapon pointed at his heart and the fact that he was unarmed, Prudence was sure that he would have leapt upon Lord Fondleton before another hateful word fell from his lips.

"I'm so sorry," she murmured toward his back so that only Lord Halthaven might hear.

George must have shifted his stance for Jasper took a step towards him, leveling the pistol.

"Do not even think about it," Jasper spat. "I have excellent aim and no qualms about shooting a man. Any challengers prior have met with an early grave."

"What sort of wretched creature are you?" Temperance muttered through her teeth.

"Be quiet," he demanded. "Make yourself useful and wake my man." Temperance hesitated, but moved to kneel beside Perry's limp form. Still, the gun remained upon the greatest threat, Lord Halthaven.

Perry groaned and rolled to his side.

"M'lord," he stammered. "My apologies."

"Ready the carriage, you drunken fool," Jasper commanded.

"M'lord, the girl ran free," Perry admitted with a grimace.

"It is no matter," Jasper said with a sly grin, "We shall still have two ladies for the trip, I think. The nuns shall just assume she abandoned their life. No one will look for her."

"I will come for them," George said in a low, dangerous tone. Prudence could not help but look up at him with wonder. After all that he had learned of her sullied condition, he would still come for her?

"I think not," Jasper replied with a lazy shrug. "You'll be dead. I don't need any witnesses muddying my name. Of course, I shall be excused for punishing the man who stole my wife and seduced her against her will... a terrible tale really. No wonder she is so addled..."

"You'll never get away with this," Prudence swore. She

would fight with every breath in her to keep Jasper from succeeding in his plans. The problem at the moment was that the three of them were neatly confined in the stall, while Jasper stood guard at the open door. If any moved to enter the aisle he would kill them with ease.

"I told you to ready the carriage!" Jasper shouted at Perry, who was still seated upon the straw-covered floor in a daze. "If I must ask again I shall designate a bullet for you as well!"

"Y-Yes, sir," the servant scampered to his feet and out the open doors at the front of the barn.

"Honestly," Jasper complained, "must I do everything myself?"

He then instructed the ladies to tie Lord Halthaven's hands and feet with the cord that had been removed from Marietta.

"Don't even think about leaving any slack," he warned. "If I suspect he might get free I'll shoot him in your sight. I am gentleman enough, otherwise, to wait until you are tucked away. It's a messy business, really, not fit for a lady's view. Now, move along. We haven't much time."

With tears in her eyes, Prudence knelt before her love unwillingly securing his bonds. If only she could communicate to him how much she loved him. George wrapped his fingers over her own and gave her a gentle squeeze. She felt as if her world would be destroyed on this day and she struggled to breathe past the lump in her throat. Lord Halthaven would die for all that he had done to help her, for loving her as well. She could not bear it.

If Jasper locked her away after all of this, she would not care. What more would there be to live for with Lord Halthaven dead, Temperance captive and Marietta abandoned once more. It was a hopeless case. In her attempt to free herself from the terrors of her life, she had placed all those she cared about in danger.

She shuddered to think of Temperance once more left to the wicked hands of a perverted gentleman. It would be all Prudence's own doing. As terrible as their father was, Jasper was a hundred times worse. The eldest of the Baggington daughters, who had thought to have escaped such terrors, would be thrust right back into the horrors of her nightmares.

Perry returned with his sniveling voice and crouched shoulders. The ladies had their hands tied together and then secured to a lead line that was removed from the tack room. Like cattle to the slaughter, they were led from the stables and bundled onto the floor of the carriage, where their bindings were increased and a gag was implemented to quiet their cries.

All hope was lost.

17

*T*he carriage swayed as the servant climbed into the driver's seat and awaited his master's return. Temperance dropped her head to Prudence's shoulder so that they might comfort one another in their distress. Prudence attempted to murmur a sound that would convey her sorrow and guilt for the situation, but Temperance just shook her head to stop her. Of course her sister was too kind to place the blame upon Prudence's shoulders, but she felt responsible just the same.

The ladies struggled against their bonds to no avail. Perry was well versed in the art of immobilization and he had taken extra care that he not lose a second prisoner in one day.

Prudence whimpered against the fabric in her mouth. She prayed that Lord Halthaven might find some way of escape.

A shot rang out in the air, and then another. A short

pause, where perhaps Jasper was checking the life source of his victim, and then a third, and final blow. The deed was done.

Prudence screamed against the cloth. Temperance raised her frightened eyes to her sister's, sadness at the loss beyond consolation. George was dead, there could be no doubt. Prudence thrashed, but could make no headway from her position on the floor of the carriage. With two tied bodies laid lengthwise there was not much room left in which to attempt to right herself.

Tears streamed freely down her face, soaking the rag in her mouth and landing upon Temperance's likewise tear-streaked features. Their sobbing must be heard from outside of the thin carriage walls, but if Perry heard it he took no mind.

The frame rocked once more, as Perry dismounted. Perhaps to help his master manage the mangled body of Lord Halthaven.

Prudence could hardly see for the tears in her eyes and the darkness of the carriage.

When the side door was thrust open, she did the only thing that she could think. She gave one swift kick into the gentleman's thigh, making firm contact with his groin and causing enough pain that he dropped away from the carriage for a moment to recover himself.

A series of deep breaths came from outside of the carriage as their captor regained his feet.

"At ease," came the low groan of a soft voice.

Prudence's head shot up at the sound. It was not Lord Fondleton's voice that spoke through the open door, but Lord Halthaven's!

She shrieked with surprise, pulling her legs back into the vehicle so that he might know that she understood.

George approached the opening with more hesitation this time, leaning forward so that the women might see his face and hear his voice before they attacked once more.

"You're safe," he said with what little breath he could draw. "It's over."

With swift fingers he released their bonds. No sooner had she been set free that Prudence threw herself into his arms. Her attack upon him was forgiven with a kiss, though it was clear that he was still in pain. Temperance had the decency to look away.

"How is it you are alive?" Prudence cried. She cupped the face of her love in her hands and kissed his lips. She did not care who saw or what they thought. She was only happy that he was alive. "I heard the shots with my own ears!"

A deep cough from the entrance to the barn had her look up into the embarrassed features of a man that she remembered from the local tavern.

"Sorry, Miss," the man grunted. "Didna' mean to intrude."

"But who are you?" Temperance asked with as much dignity as could be managed. A second male, younger than the first, stepped from the stables as well. Both had rifles tucked against their shoulders and disgruntled but satisfied looks upon their faces.

"We 'ad business with that bloke inside," the younger stated. "Done wrong by my sisters, 'e did."

"Three daughters I've got," the elder explained, "just

in the village next. I keep a tavern you see and that rake had mind to ruin 'em all, but I made it right. I swore I would make it right."

"He's dead?" Prudence gasped. "Jasper's dead?"

"Sure as the evening stars," the barkeep nodded. "I shot him twice myself and my son finished 'im off. Found this gent all tied in the stall and 'e seemed alright so we released 'im. Your man raced straight out 'ere to you ladies and some scrawny fellow ran off before we could tell 'im what for."

Prudence could not believe her ears. Jasper was dead. His terrible ways had caught up with him at last and he had paid the ultimate price. She was free of him. The world was free of him.

"If you don' mind, Miss, we ought to make ourselves scarce before the magistrate hears word of what 'appened 'ere." He tipped his hat and shifted his rifle to the other shoulder. "Would be awfully kind if you three were to recall some highwaymen. Save me a load of trouble."

Lord Halthaven assured them that he would take care of the matter and the pair walked off into the woods never to be seen again.

Prudence just stood in silence, terrified of what she knew lay in the barn and yet overcome with the knowledge that the horror was over at last.

"Well," Temperance said with a shrug, "you make a fine widow."

Prudence turned to her sister with confusion.

"What?" she asked. How could her sister be so blasé at a time like this? Temperance even had the gall to smile. It was unbefitting of one poised to be made a nun.

"Prudence, don't you understand?" Temperance asked.

Prudence shook her head.

"No one need know anything, but that Lord Fondleton met a terrible end of his own wicked making," Temperance grasped her sister's shoulders so that she might impress the truth upon her. "Who are we to say otherwise? You are now the grieving Widow Fondleton and no longer need to hide yourself. You can stop running! You're free!"

Her jaw grew slack as she realized what her sister was saying. Not only was Prudence free of her husband, but she would also remain an incredibly wealthy widow. She turned her head and looked into the glowing face of Lord Halthaven. She knew not what to say.

"You shall have to mourn for a bit," he said with a slight smile, "just to be sure there is no question."

She nodded.

"I can do that."

"Perhaps by Michaelmas you could pay a visit to your old friend, the Baron Halthaven," Temperance teased. "I hear he is in search of a wife."

"You two are terrible!" Prudence attempted a scolding tone, but could not contain the smile that had spread across her face. In an instant, the entire forecast of her future had turned upon its head. Prudence laughed with a mixture of relief and what she was sure was hysteria.

The dream of life at Halthaven could be made a reality. Marietta was safe and would be kept so for the rest of her days, and Prudence could be with George. It did not seem real. Even Temperance seemed more than pleased with the sudden turn of events, though Prudence could not fully understand why.

She asked her sister as much.

"It is only that..." Temperance bit her lip with an excited grin that she hadn't revealed in years, "with father gone... I may return home."

"Home?" Prudence said with surprise.

"I never was much suited for the abbey," Temperance admitted. "It is far too quiet for my liking."

Prudence recalled that Temperance had been dragging her feet when it came to taking her vows. Now she understood why. Though her sister had resigned herself to life in the abbey she had not fully convinced herself that she belonged, nor that she could remain devoted to the life.

"Oh no!" Prudence said with a groan, "Reverend Mother shall be so cross with me! I swore not to divert you!"

Temperance laughed.

"Not at all," she replied. "I have a feeling the Mother Abbess has suspected all along. Only, she hoped that I might grow into it. I tried, I did. I even kept from reading all of your letters so that I might forget, but it was not to be."

"Is it wrong that I feel happy?" Prudence asked in a small voice.

Lord Halthaven tucked her beneath his arm and pulled her against him.

"I think you both have been long overdue for some happiness," he said. "Soon enough, it shall be my duty to ensure. A task I greatly look forward to."

"Truly?" Prudence looked up at him with concern. "You are not mortified by all that you heard of me? I'm ruined, you know. There is much that he... that I..." she gestured at her body as if to encompass the flaws within her being.

In reply, Lord Halthaven pressed a kiss to the top of her head.

"I care nothing for that," He whispered into her hair. "There is nothing you could do and nothing that poor excuse for a man could say that would make me love you any less, my dear Prudence. Only can you be happy?" he asked. "Was there truth in his words that you could never be so? I don't believe it, but tell me true."

"I *am* happy," she replied. "I am happy when I am with you."

"Then that is all the answer I require," he said.

EPILOGUE

*I*t was not long after the turn of the year that Lady Fondleton became Lady Halthaven. The late earl's estate was sold and passed to some other titled gentleman who would take his place and, hopefully, bring some light to the dark past that had occurred there.

As for Prudence, she never wished to set foot upon those wretched grounds again. The newly made Lady Halthaven was perfectly happy in her little wood with the rose-lined path. The roses, she would later discover were a myriad of colors that transformed the lane into the most beautiful summer picture that Marietta would never tire of painting.

The young girl was most pleased to hear that Prudence would become a permanent fixture in their home. In the evenings, she slept peaceful and protected with her growing pup to keep guard. Not that any of the three need worry again about such an adventure. With

Lord Fondleton's death the entire countryside became a safer place for lady-folk in general.

Prudence never saw the barkeep or his son again. Once, when passing through the neighboring village, she and her husband considered stopping to offer their patronage, but decided that it was best to be done with that part of their life as a whole.

Besides, the couple agreed that it would be best to steer clear, for the highwaymen that had murdered Prudence's late husband had yet to be captured. Not that anyone ever put much effort into the search.

For the first time in her life, Prudence looked forward to the prospect of having a child of her own. She had no fear that her husband might bring harm to a daughter. She had seen well enough that Lord Halthaven was a kind and compassionate caretaker to all that fell under his domain. For the first time Prudence was happy and this time she knew it was forever.

CONTINUE READING FOR A SNEAK PEEK OF...

Almost Promised ~ Temperance
by Isabella Thorne

*M*iss Temperance Baggington stared up at the sign as it threatened to free itself from its brackets and fly away upon the windstorm that was whipping its way through the streets of Upper Nettlefold.

"You have brought the devil of a storm with you!" A feminine laugh came from the street behind her and startled Temperance from her pondering. She turned to look upon the woman whose namesake the sign declared. Mrs. Cordelia Hardcastle, owner and proprietress of Hardcastle House, stepped through the gate and beckoned that Temperance follow.

The woman was used to strange ladies landing upon her doorstep. Temperance recalled that Mrs. Hardcastle often took on waifs and gave aid and employment to those in need. Mrs. Hardcastle's prickly demeanor hid a soft heart and kind spirit.

"Come, come," Mrs. Hardcastle called as she hastened her unidentified arrival up the step and through the door. "The entire town has hunkered down for the storm. We've no reason to linger before it releases its fury upon us."

Temperance offered a thankful nod from beneath her hood and did as she was bid. It had been years since she had last set foot upon the streets of Upper Nettlefold. Five long years to be exact. The foyer looked just as she recalled when she had raced to Mrs. Hardcastle on that last and final day, seeking salvation.

The woman had helped her then. Temperance was certain that she could count on a warm cup of tea and a room for the night; at least until she worked up the courage to do what she must. Even now, she was not certain that she should have come. The prospect of returning to her family home, after all of these years, was daunting.

Of course, the object of her trepidation was no longer in residence. Her father was gone from the earth. She cautioned herself to not speak ill of the dead, but she could not quell ill thoughts. She whispered a prayer of penitence.

Five years spent with the good sisters of the Halthurst Abbey had taught her patience, but they could not quite instill humility. Nor could they take away the stain her father's brutality had left in her.

Mrs. Hardcastle called for the cook, who relieved the proprietress of the overflowing basket of goods that she carried upon her arm. Mrs. Hardcastle waved Temperance into the sitting room and requested the aforementioned tray of tea and biscuits to be brought. Sensing her companion was not yet prepared to reveal her identity, Mrs. Hardcastle waited until they were alone before she shed her cloak and held out her hand to accept Temperance's wrap to hang as well.

Temperance took a deep breath before easing the fabric of the hood away from her face. The resounding gasp was not unexpected, though it did little to settle her nerves.

"Good Lord, Miss Baggington," Mrs. Hardcastle crossed herself and asked forgiveness, "Oh, I beg your pardon Sister Temperance, you would be now, or did you take a saint's name for your own, Sister?"

"Not at all, Mrs. Hardcastle," Temperance muttered. "I am no nun. I found I could not complete the vows, though I will forever be grateful for your facilitation of my acceptance into Halthurst Abbey."

Mrs. Hardcastle clucked at Temperance to hand over her cloak so that it might be hung to dry. "Not another word until we've sat proper," she instructed. "I should say we'd best start at the beginning."

"Yes, ma'am," Temperance obliged. She had no belongings save the thick woolen sheath dress that covered her thin frame and a paper-wrapped bundle that she settled beneath a nearby bench. The abbey kept its own flock from which to make the woolen cloth. Temperance had grown used to the coarse fabric after all these years. She had nearly forgotten what a muslin gown might feel like against her skin.

She recalled a fine silk and velvet blend that her mother had commissioned from London before she had made her escape. Temperance had worn it once, on the evening she had been made to meet the gentleman that she had been promised to marry. The gown had been a dream; the gentleman, a nightmare. Temperance shuddered with the thought.

"Oh my dear, you are chilled," Mrs. Hardcastle said misjudging the reason for her tremors.

Just as the tray was delivered, the storm let loose with a vengeance. Mrs. Hardcastle moved to the window to pull the curtains shut against the draft.

"There now," she clapped her hands. "No need to let the dreary outside spoil the inside. I must admit that you were the last person I expected to see upon my doorstep."

"Yes, well, in the light of... recent events..." Temperance trailed off.

She did not know how to say the words over the lump that had appeared in her throat. She felt as if she might choke on it. Mrs. Hardcastle took note of her guest's discomfort and moved to pour the tea so that Temperance might recover. Temperance took a long draught of the scalding liquid and found that the warmth that trailed down her throat, and through the center of her body, did give her strength.

"With recent events being as they are," she continued, "I thought I might attempt a visit."

"Yes," Mrs. Hardcastle nodded. "I assume you are referring to the death of your father, the Viscount Mortel . Strange thing, that," she said with a vague nod into her own cup. "It all came on so sudden. Had I known you hadn't taken your vows I would have written straight away."

"I tried," Temperance explained. "Again and again, I tried. It never did seem right. I couldn't do it."

Mrs. Hardcastle pierced Temperance with a reprimanding look. "What didn't seem right? Taking the vows or writing to your family?"

Temperance lowered her head and whispered. "I couldn't. What if he..."

Mrs. Hardcastle interrupted. "Your family seems to think it done, and you made a proper member of the abbey," she scolded. "Have you not written to them in all these years? Not even to your sisters?"

Temperance shook her head. "I asked the Mother Abbess to burn their letters. She didn't, of course. She kept them with the hope that I might ask for them one day, but I couldn't bear it. It was better to have a clean cut, else I might have been tempted to return for my sisters' sakes."

"Do not go feeling badly about that," Mrs. Hardcastle instructed. "I can see that you do. You have no reason for such self-infliction. You were right to think of yourself for once. Those years of trying to shelter your siblings only made it worse for you. You could have never kept him from the others once they came of age, especially not once you had been married off to that brainless oaf."

"I thought it best that everyone think I only wished to avoid the marriage." Temperance hung her head as she recalled the frightened child she had once been. She was still frightened, only less of a child.

"It was long ago," Mrs. Hardcastle soothed.

"But I remember like it was yesterday," she whispered. "I preferred to keep the rumors to my own name, rather than burden the family. Still," she shuddered, "I knew when Father said I was to marry his old friend that I would never be free of him...of either of them. They had some sort of... arrangement, I suspect, to... to... because Father did not want to lose..."

Mrs. Hardcastle swore under her breath. She was not one prone to profanity and so the effect was all the more significant to express her disgust.

"My blood still boils as much as that first day you told me of your troubles." The older woman bit into a biscuit with a vengeance. "Curse your father and may he rot below. Never was there a gentleman who deserved eternal flames more than he."

Temperance agreed, though she had yet to be so vocal in her opinions as the independent Mrs. Hardcastle. The good sisters would never allow such. The abbess had indeed told Temperance to pray for her father's soul, and she had done so, but she could not help but think he deserved damnation for the hell he visited upon his own daughters. Still, such thoughts should not creep into prayers.

"I promised you he would not get away with it forever," Mrs. Hardcastle nodded. "I will not lie. I paid a visit to your mother after your departure and plied her with some of my homemade wine. She missed you terribly, but was relieved to know that I had sent you someplace safe. She was well into the bottle when she finally spoke of the matter herself."

"She told you?"

Mrs. Hardcastle nodded.

Temperance hung on her every word. She had not spoken to her mother since the day that she ran away without warning. All that had happened since was news to her. "What did she say?" Temperance asked.

"I've never seen a lady more like a fountain than your mother. I suspect years of holding in the pain came forth at once." Mrs. Hardcastle clucked once more. "Of course she knew I could be trusted, just as you knew. Still, she was terribly afraid of him, with good reason.

Afraid for herself and her children, she was. She was happy you were free, but her hands were tied with the other girls. She knew she had to get the rest of them out of that manor, so she threw herself into the marriages. Now that did not work out so well for Miss Prudence, but there was naught to be done in that case, what with her having been caught in an embrace. At the time, I thought it a blessing.

Prudence would be quickly married and away from your father. Her new husband being an earl meant that her father, as a lesser member of the peerage, could not touch her. Of course, that was before I started asking questions as to the nature of the Earl of Fondleton.

I can tell you this: I did not like what I discovered. By then, it was too late I'm afraid. Lord Fondleton had some shady dealings that he kept well below the notice of proper society. A wicked rake of a man and a swindler to boot."

Temperance bowed her head and mumbled some halfhearted comment in memory of the late Lord Fondleton.

"Hold your tongue," Mrs. Hardcastle scolded. "Jasper Numbton was as bad as they come. Poor Prudence fell from one beast's trap and straight into another. Bless her poor little heart, a widow at such a young age."

Temperance nodded. "Still, it all worked out in the end."

"That it did." Mrs. Hardcastle shook her head with a smile.

Though the older lady did not know the entire story; there were few that did. It was clear that Prudence was happy to move on from the loss of her first husband. Some still called her "*the baggage*" and said such a lack of decorum was expected of a woman such as Prudence, but they did not know the truth.

Desperation does strange things to a person. Temperance knew Prudence was indeed despairing when she arrived at Halthurst Abbey, bedraggled and frantic. No one could blame Prudence if they knew the true story. Prudence had mourned for the appropriate time and now it was whispered that the wealthy widow Fondleton had already made a connection to the Baron Halthaven who lived in the North. It would not be long, rumor had it, before she would be happily remarried, or at least Temperance hoped it was so. Prudence deserved happiness.

"I cannot believe that Mother told you about Father!" Temperance turned the conversation back with a look of awe. "She made us all swear never to tell a soul. It would ruin us and the family. She was certain if we told anyone, father would make a claim for *scandalum magnatum*. My brother would lose his inheritance and the manor and... well all sorts of trouble, I'm sure.

She especially did not want the boys to learn of it. I

did always wonder if they had their suspicions, but we all did well to keep silent. Thankfully the boys were often away at Eton, and later making visits to their friends. Besides," she added, "it would not do to incite Father's wrath. He was cruel even to my brothers; only not in the same way as the girls."

The Baggington sisters were blessed with four brothers. With protection of their position in mind, the five daughters, along with their mother, had done what was necessary to keep the truth below the notice of the gentlemen of the *Ton*. There was nothing that destroyed the families of the peerage faster than internal disputes.

Temperance shuddered to think what Isaac, the eldest and newly proclaimed Viscount Mortel, would have done. A confrontation with his father would have had him stripped of his inheritance, title and future without hesitation, she was sure, but he was away at school when the abuse had started and none of the women ventured to tell Isaac on the rare occasions he visited home. The late Viscount Mortel was not above using his clout to enforce his rule. His sons had walked in his shadow, doing their best to keep their heads low and his approval at hand.

"The entire situation was a mess from the off," Mrs. Hardcastle grumbled. "If I had had my way..." she trailed off. "Well, let's just say it would have been handled sooner."

"Sooner?" Temperance asked. She was afraid to press further into the implication that it had been *handled* at all.

"The Lord works in mysterious ways," Mrs.

Hardcastle smiled. "Look at Lord Fondleton, Providence sorted him out as well."

Temperance did not know how to respond. Neither Providence, nor The Lord, had sorted out the Earl of Fondleton, but Temperance kept her own council on the matter. It did not take much thought to realize that Jasper Numbton was long overdue for a confrontation. Temperance would not speak on that tale, however, for there was much there that was to best secret. Her own, as well as her sister's.

"Now," Mrs. Hardcastle continued without pause, "does your family know of your return?"

"No," Temperance admitted. "I was hoping that I could stay here until I work up the courage to make myself known to them."

Mrs. Hardcastle shook her head and pursed her lips. "I am full to bursting at the moment," she explained. "I even had to pair up some of my girls. Even if I had the room, you know what I would say."

Temperance nodded. Mrs. Hardcastle could always be relied on for firm and fair advice. Temperance had wondered if she would turn her away from the start. It was Temperance own indecision that was keeping her here when there was more than enough room at the manor. And, she kept reminding herself, her father was no longer there to darken the doorway. The thought made her feel rather giddy.

"Chin up, child," the boarding house matron said with a bolstering grin. "You've no one left to fear anymore."

"I know," Temperance worried. "But shall they accept me?"

She had run away without a word, without correspondence for five years. If it had not been for the recent arrival of her sister Prudence at the abbey she might have never spoken to her family again. The knowledge of her father's passing had changed everything for Temperance. In that moment, she had finally felt hope.

"For heaven's sake child," Mrs. Hardcastle laughed. "You lived in a religious institution for five years. Have you not heard the story of the prodigal son?"

"Of course I have," Temperance replied.

"Then you know that you shall be welcomed home again with open arms," the elder woman advised. "And if they do not accept you, then come back to me, and I will give them all a piece of my mind!"

Temperance could not help but laugh at the rock of strength that was Mrs. Hardcastle. There were rumors that she had once had a tragic history of her own, though no one knew the exact nature of the tale. Still, whatever had happened had built an iron resolve in the woman that left her without fear.

Temperance wished that one day she might be as confident as her benefactress. Though she still trembled with nerves at the thought of meeting her family after five long years, Temperance began to feel encouraged by Mrs. Hardcastle's confidence.

They agreed that Temperance would stay through dinner, to wait out the storm, and then the boarding house driver would take her along the winding road to

Mortel Manor which lay outside of the bustling town of Upper Nettlefold.

❧

CONTINUE READING....

Almost Promised ~ Temperance
by Isabella Thorne

WANT EVEN MORE REGENCY ROMANCE...

Follow Isabella Thorne on BookBub
https://www.bookbub.com/profile/isabella-thorne

Sign up for my VIP Reader List!
at
https://isabellathorne.com/

Receive weekly updates from Isabella and an
EXCLUSIVE FREE STORY

Like Isabella Thorne on Facebook
https://www.facebook.com/isabellathorneauthor/

Printed in Great Britain
by Amazon